crush stuff.

crush stuff.

a girl stuff novel

lisi harrison

G. P. PUTNAM'S SONS

G. P. PUTNAM'S SONS
An imprint of Penguin Random House LLC, New York

alloyentertainment

Produced by Alloy Entertainment • 30 Hudson Yards, 22nd floor
New York, NY 10001

Visit us online at penguinrandomhouse.com

Library of Congress Cataloging-in-Publication Data
Names: Harrison, Lisi, author.
Title: Crush stuff: a girl stuff novel / Lisi Harrison.
Description: New York: G. P. Putnam's Sons, 2021. | Series: Girl stuff; book 2 |
Summary: "Seventh-grade besties Fonda, Drew, and Ruthie navigate crushes and friend
drama as they plan for their seventh-grade overnight school trip"—Provided by publisher.
Identifiers: LCCN 2021015737 (print) | LCCN 2021015738 (ebook) |
ISBN 9781984815019 (trade paperback) | ISBN 9781984815002 (ebook)
Subjects: CYAC: Friendship—Fiction. | Love—Fiction. | School field trips—Fiction. |
Middle schools—Fiction. | Schools—Fiction.
Classification: LCC PZ7.H2527 Cr 2021 (print) | LCC PZ7.H2527 (ebook) | DDC [Fic]—dc23
LC record available at https://lccn.loc.gov/2021015737
LC ebook record available at https://lccn.loc.gov/2021015738

Printed in the United States of America
ISBN 9781984815019
1 3 5 7 9 10 8 6 4 2
LSCH

Design by Suki Boynton • Text set in Freight Text Pro

⚔

For my crush, Wyatt, who fed me, loved me,
and supported me while I wrote this novel.
(I hope we're still together by the time
this publishes. If not, I might have to name
book three Awkward Stuff.)

chapter one.

IN THE MOVIES, Halloween season—or what boring people call October—is depicted by howling wind, skeletal tree branches, and creeping shadows. But in Poplar Creek, California, where wind is more of a lazy sigh, palm fronds sway like a fresh blowout, and the sun is too bright for shadows, Halloween season ushers in a different type of terror, one that Fonda Miller named the Seventh-Grade Slopover.

"The Ferdink Farms field trip is pure hell," Fonda said as she, Drew, and Ruthie walked home from Poplar Middle School. It was Friday, and the next-door besties, or nesties, as they called themselves, were spending the night at Fonda's. Her stride should have had spring, her steps pep. But the feet in her leopard-print high-tops were heavy with dread because this year's Seventh-Grade Slopover would be no different than last year's Sixth-Grade Slopover. And no different was no bueno.

"How bad can it be?" Ruthie asked, her wide blue eyes beaming optimism. And who could blame her? The students in the Talented and Gifted program were also invited. Which meant that for three days and two nights, Ruthie and her TAG friends would have the same schedule as Fonda and Drew. It was something Ruthie had always wanted. It was something they had all wanted. But not like this.

"Two nights, three days, and seven meals of nothing but pig slop. That's how bad." Fonda removed the mirrored heart-shaped sunglasses she'd "borrowed" from her sister Amelia so they could see the panic in her eyes. "We shovel horse poo, milk cows, and sleep on mattresses that smell like oily grandfather scalp."

"My grandfather is bald, so his scalp doesn't smell oily," Ruthie said. "His has more of a minty smell. Hey, maybe my mattress will smell minty!"

"Then mine will smell like sticky notes," Drew said, because her Grandpa Lou tacked Post-it reminders all over the house so her Grandma Mae wouldn't forget anything.

"I bet Weird-O's mattress is gonna smell like money," Fonda said, pointing at the boy who lived at the top of their street. He was ambling up his driveway, shoulders rounded and neck arched, as he thumbed the screen of his phone. His rich, preppy, private-school look—button-down shirt, white sneakers, and corn-tortilla-colored slacks—might be on point in Connecticut or, say, Boston—but it completely missed the point in California. Everything about Weird-O missed the point.

"His name is Owen Lowell-Kline," Ruthie said, defending him as usual. Not because she liked Owen, or even really knew him. But because two years earlier, he bought her entire supply of Girl Scout cookies, which freed her up to go to the beach with Fonda and Drew. "I feel bad for him."

"Why?" Drew asked. "Because he ate fifty boxes of Do-si-dos?"

"They weren't *all* Do-si-dos. There were Samoas and Tagalongs too. And, no. I feel bad for Owen because he doesn't have any friends."

"Because he's a pick-me," Fonda said. If Ruthie had ever had the misfortune of being in class with Owen and witnessed him waving his hand at the teacher while shouting, "Pick me, pick me," she would have felt bad for *herself*, not Owen.

"Just because he's a pick-me doesn't mean you have to be a pick-on-him," Ruthie said. Then she laughed. Everyone did. Because it was one of the clunkiest comebacks of all time.

The laughter stopped the moment Fonda's mother greeted them in the kitchen and asked how her day was. "Tell me everything," Joan said, her russet-brown eyes wide and eager.

She was a feminist studies professor at UC Irvine and didn't teach on Fridays, which freed her up to serve snacks and pry at the end of every week. "Kitchen time" was something Fonda looked forward to. But not today. Today, Fonda didn't want to relive the details; she wanted to forget them and get right to the snacks.

She opened the pantry and grabbed three bags of cheese popcorn. "They announced the Slopover today."

"What's a slopover?" Joan asked. She set out three glasses on the table for the girls and filled them with chocolate almond milk. "And why do you seem so miserable about it?"

"We have to scoop horse poo," Ruthie said.

"And sleep on mattresses that smell like oily grandfather scalp," Drew added.

"Ew, are you talking about Ferdink Farms?" Winfrey asked as she padded barefoot into the kitchen. She was wearing a wet suit, unzipped to reveal her midriff, and a red bikini top. Knowing her, she probably wore that to school. And if she did, it wouldn't be long before every junior at Poplar Creek High began wearing it too. Because Fonda's sixteen-year-old sister, with her butterscotch-colored highlights, cactus-green eyes, and three first-place surf trophies, was major like that.

"Ferdink Farms is still a thing?" said Amelia, the middle Miller sister, who was also wearing a bikini, but no wet suit. She entered behind Winfrey, piling a mess of fiery auburn waves on top of her head. A freshman in high school, she was a star volleyball player with a statement sunglass collection that could fill a swimming pool. So yeah, she was pretty major too. "I thought that dump burned in last year's wildfire."

"Nope," Fonda sighed. "The fire didn't want it either."

"Smart fire," Winfrey said. Then to her mother, "Joan, can I borrow the car? Amelia and I are going to the beach."

"Really?" Joan took a seat at the table. "This isn't like you."

"Um, Mother, have we met? Amelia and I surf every Friday after school."

"I was talking to Fonda," Joan said, hands serious and clasped.

"Ew, why would you do that?"

Fonda ignored her sister's jab. "What isn't like me?"

"Civic laziness," Joan said.

Fonda had no clue what "civic laziness" meant, but she *did* know that she was about to get lectured on feminism or activism or both. Every conversation with her mother went there eventually. "If you don't agree with your leader's choices, speak up. The world is only going to change if you change it."

Fonda nearly choked on her chocolate almond milk. "How am I supposed to do *that*?"

"Real change, enduring change, happens one step at a time."

Ruthie smacked the table like a game-show buzzer. "Ruth Bader Ginsburg!"

"That's right." Joan beamed. "Very good, Ruthie."

"I'm a huge fan."

Joan beamed even brighter. "Who isn't?"

"Um, I'm not," Winfrey said. "Unless Ruth Bader Ginsburg is the name of your car."

"You have a voice, Fonda. Don't use it to complain. Use it to campaign!"

Ruthie hit the table again. "Gloria Steinem!"

"No," Joan said.

"Tarana Burke?"

"Nope."

"Malala?"

"No, Ruthie. That one was Joan Miller."

"You?"

Joan nodded proudly.

Ruthie got out of her chair, sat on Joan's lap like a toddler visiting Santa, and hugged her. "JM, you are my everything."

"This popcorn is *my* everything," Drew said, crumpling her bag. "Can we have seconds?"

"Check the pantry," Fonda said impatiently. Because now what? Her mother didn't give her a plan; she gave her *words*. The type of words that end up on bumper stickers, tea bags, and motivational Instagram posts. A wildfire couldn't quash Ferdink Farms, and Joan thought some Ruth Bader Ginsburg quote was the answer? "Mom, what am I supposed to do? Stand outside the principal's office with a sign that says *Hell no, we won't go?*"

"I don't think we should say *hell*," Drew called from inside the pantry. "*Heck* might be better."

"Mom!" Winfrey said with a stomp of her bare foot. "The keys!"

"Slogans don't work because they don't offer a solution," Joan said. "Instead of shouting about what you don't want, try shouting about what you do want."

What do I want? Fonda asked herself. It was a good question. One that she didn't know how to answer. She definitely wanted an overnight field trip, especially now that Drew and Ruthie were going too. But what kind of field trip? And where?

"I don't want a place that smells like horse poo," she began.

Drew returned to the table with three new bags of popcorn. "Isn't that more of what you don't want?"

"Exactly!" Joan smacked the table. "What *do* you want?"

Fonda stood. She thought better on her feet. "I want a place that smells like fresh air. I want a place with fun activities. I want a place with good food and candy. I want—"

"What about Catalina Island?" Amelia said. Then she grabbed the chocolate almond milk off the table and began chugging it from the carton.

"Great call!" Winfrey said. "Catalina's all those things. How rad was the Fourth?" she asked Amelia, who, unlike Fonda, was "cool enough" to party with Winfrey's friends.

"So rad."

"Right?"

"Right."

"And the ferry ride is super rad too."

"So super rad."

"Right?"

"Right."

"Girls, details *please*," Joan insisted. "Use your words."

Winfrey lifted herself onto the countertop and began swinging her legs. "They have snorkeling, zip lines, an ice cream shop—"

"And wild bison," Amelia added.

"Wild is good," Ruthie said. "No poop to scoop!"

Fonda stopped pacing. They were right. Catalina Island would be perfect. And to think it was right there in front of her the whole time. Literally. Less than forty miles off the coast, it rose up from the Pacific Ocean like a sleeping sea monster's spine.

If Fonda upgraded the class trip, not only would the entire seventh grade worship her, she'd have Catalina stories to swap with her sisters. She'd be known as a civically unlazy game changer who single-handedly put an end to the Slopover. Fonda Miller would matter. The nesties would matter. Her social life would finally be worth living.

"I'm going to do it!" she announced.

"Great," Winfrey said. "Now, Joan, can I please have the car keys?"

Fonda spotted them by the banana basket and quietly swiped them. Then she dangled them in front of Winfrey's face like a hypnotist's watch. "Only if you drop us at Fresh & Fruity. Fro-yo helps me think."

"Seriously?" Winfrey screeched. She turned to her mother, hoping for backup. As always, Joan looked away, refusing to get involved.

"Come on," Fonda said. "Please—"

Before she could finish her request, or even begin it, Amelia snatched the keys from Fonda's hand and tossed them to Winfrey. "Let's ride!"

As her sisters ran out of the house, cackling victoriously, Fonda, who would have normally felt like a stage-five loser in that moment, kept her head held high. Drew and Ruthie were looking at her with chocolate almond milk mustaches, ready for their marching orders. They were going to dismantle a tradition and overthrow the status quo. If they did their jobs right, the real stage-five loser would be Ferdink Farms. And if they didn't? Fonda would be doomed to inhale the stench of her Ferdink failure with every scoop of horse poop those farmers made her shovel.

chapter two.

"WHAT DO YOU mean you can't leave?" Drew asked her brother, Doug, as he emerged from the dressing room at Poplar Surf and Sport with an armload of board shorts and skinny jeans. "I skated here because you said you'd be off work at three."

"That was before Colter called in sick and stuck me with his shift." He dumped the pile by the T-shirt display and sighed. "Why doesn't anyone clean up after themselves?" His blond hair was moussed into spikes that mirrored his prickly mood. "I mean, how hard is it to fold a pair of jeans?"

"Really hard, I guess," Drew said. "Or you wouldn't be so bummed about it."

"I'm bummed because I wanted to skate, and now I'm here until six."

"Six?"

The bell on the shop door rang, and in walked Will Wilder with a girl wearing a green trucker hat that said SKATE HAIR, DON'T CARE. Doug's schedule no longer mattered. Drew's sweaty armpits, blushing cheeks, shaky hands, and raging jealousy suddenly did. She quickly slipped behind the rack of wet suits and evaluated her crush's mysterious companion: cutoff denim short shorts, an unbuttoned flannel shirt, and a yellow one-piece bathing suit. Long dark hair, fuchsia streaks, mouth full of bubble gum . . . She had a dangerous air about her. Nothing that threatened Drew's sense of safety, just her sense of self.

"Dude, what are you doing behind the wet suits?" Doug asked, loud as lunchtime.

"Shhh."

Technically, Drew had no right to be jealous. It wasn't like she and Will were a thing. Or even kind of a thing. Yes, he'd admitted he liked her at Ava G.'s boy-girl party two weekends ago. And, yes, she fully L'ed him back. But that was before Will found out Drew had called him a doozer (dude loser). Before he heard she wouldn't cross the road to help him, even if he was injured. Before misunderstanding poked a hole in their L bubble and all the awesome seeped out.

Granted, Drew didn't mean any of those things. She was beyond upset when she said them, and for good reason. She and Will had flirt-bonded on the last day of Battleflag Family Camp, and then, when they saw each other at school, he ignored her. So, yeah, Drew said some things she didn't mean. But she apologized. She even proved she'd cross the road for him when he was injured. Because when Will wiped out on his skateboard, she hurried across Fontana Avenue, rushed to his side, and cleaned his wound like the professional nurse she was determined to become.

Did he forgive her on the spot and resume L'ing her? Not exactly. But he ignored her a little less. He waved when they passed each other in the halls, smiled when he saw her at the crosswalk, and playfully called her backside 180s "buttside 180s" when they ran into each other at the skate park. But that was it. And "it" wasn't enough.

"Excuse me," said the mysterious girl, her head now

poking through the wet suits. "Do you sell microwaves?"

"Uh, no," Drew stammered.

"Then what's with all the *short* boards?"

The girl and Will busted out laughing. Drew rolled her eyes. Did she really just fall for that dad joke? It was older than Kelly Slater.

"Hilarious," Drew said flatly as she stepped through the curtain of rubber-scented neoprene.

"Oh, hey," Will said, his denim-blue eyes lightening as his cheeks darkened. "You work here?"

"No. My brother does. We were supposed to go skating but—" She shrugged. "Whatever." She wasn't in the mood to share the details. Drew *was* in the mood, however, to know if Will L'ed the dad-joker more than he L'ed her.

"So, uh, what are you doing?" The question was meant for Will, but Drew's attention happened to be on the girl when she asked it.

"Hiding from Henry," she said, which sent them into another annoying fit of laughter.

"Keelie tried to tell him that his wallet was falling out of his shorts and that he'd lose all his money if he wasn't careful," Will said. "He wouldn't listen, so—"

"I stole it!" Keelie proudly waved the checkered wallet as proof.

"We bolted before he noticed," Will added. "He's across the street looking for us now."

"I say we go to Fresh & Fruity and get some fro-yo," Keelie said. "Henry's treat, of course."

"I love that place," Drew said, forcing her way into their private little world. "I even have a coupon for it." She quickly cringed. Who bragged about coupons? Especially the kind that are only valid on Mondays between noon and four p.m.

"I have one of those!" Will said. His expression warmed the way it did back at Battleflag, when they realized they both loved that old movie *The Skateboard Kid*. "But it's only good on Mondays."

"Same!" Drew giggled a little as her next thought took shape. It was risky and bold—daring, even. "We should go on Monday," she tried. "You know, before it expires."

"Totally!" Keelie said, as if she suddenly had a coupon too. Which she probably didn't. If she did, why would she be stealing wallets?

"Works for me," Will said.

"Same," said Keelie's annoying mouth.

"So, Monday it is?"

"Monday it is." Will smiled, just as Bob Marley's "One Love" began playing over the stereo.

Drew smiled back. Bob didn't know how right he was.

chapter three.

RUTHIE GOLDMAN UNFURLED her dancing-pineapples towel on the sand, sprayed her body with SPF 100— twice—then lowered her visor to block the afternoon rays. Mother Nature had definitely put the *sun* in this Sunday, and for the first time in forever, Ruthie wasn't hating the beach. As an outdoor-reading enthusiast, she preferred gloomy, overcast days—no page glare, no dripping sweat to blur her vision, no pressure to stop midchapter and jump in the ocean. But today, Ruthie didn't even *want* to lose herself in a make-believe world. Today, she liked the real-life sunny one. Because today, her three-person friend group had grown to four. What was once odd was now even. And that meant they could finally play charades.

"I just downloaded the Renaissance edition," said Sage Silverman, Ruthie's closest friend in the Talented and Gifted program. She was the first person the nesties had ever welcomed into their tight group, and Ruthie was beyond grateful. No more straddling two worlds, dividing her time, or missing out. Like the pink Swiss Multitool Ruthie won for selling the most Girl Scout cookies (thanks to her hungry neighbor Owen Lowell-Kline), everything she needed was in one convenient place.

Fonda propped herself up on her elbows, her expression salted in confusion. "Renaissance edition?"

Sage propped herself up too, intentionally mirroring Fonda. Rhea, their TAG teacher, was a huge fan of the technique. *The idea is to assume the same body position as the person you're talking to,* Rhea had explained, *thereby putting them at ease and letting them know, subconsciously, of course, that you are interested in what they're saying.*

It was a clever move by Sage, considering she used to call "typical learners" like Fonda and Drew dumb-dumbs. Ever since Ruthie had made it clear that *dumb-*

dumb was an off-limits term, Sage tried not to act all judgy and intellectually superior. Most of the time she succeeded. Other times, not so much.

"The Renaissance, Fonda, was a fervent period of European cultural, artistic, political, and economic rebirth following the Middle Ages. Generally described as taking place from the fourteenth century to the seventeenth century."

"Fun, right?" Ruthie clapped. Because how one was supposed to pantomime *Michelangelo* was anyone's guess. "I'll run up to Circle K and get some pens. I already have paper in my backpack, so—"

"Pens?" Drew pulled her blond ponytail through the back of her new green trucker hat. "Why would we need those?"

"To write down our topics, nerd," Ruthie said.

"You're the nerd," Drew teased. "Writing is for boomers."

"No, you're the nerd," Ruthie fired back. "How are you going to know what to act out if we don't write it down?"

Fonda, Sage, and Drew indicated their phones.

"The Charades app," Sage said. A gaggle of teeny-bikini-wearing high school girls sauntered by, butt cheeks fully exposed. "Dumb-dumbs," she whispered so only Ruthie could hear.

"Ugh, I can't take it anymore!" Fonda announced.

"Agreed," Sage said with a toss of her pink-dyed hair. "Those girls are so desperate for attention, am I right?" She glanced down at her peach-colored one-piece to make sure she was fully covered.

Fonda rolled onto her stomach and buried her head in a mound of bunched-up clothes.

"I'm talking about the Ruthie situation."

"Me? What did I do?"

"*You* didn't do anything," Fonda clarified. "It's your parents. When are they going to let you out of no-cell hell and into the twenty-first century?"

Drew giggled. "It would make planning things a lot easier."

"Right?" Sage said. "I mean, Ruthie, how do you research or listen to podcasts or follow the news?"

"I'm not a philistine, Sage. I have a laptop." But Ruthie knew they were right. How many times had she sat on the sidelines while her friends shared fun facts, made last-minute plans, or laughed at a TikTok? She *was* in no-cell hell.

Sage popped the top of a Bai lemonade. "So you don't even want one?"

"I do. It's just that my dad thinks they're addicting and my mom's afraid the radio frequency energy will melt my orbitofrontal cortex."

"When's the last time you asked them?" Fonda asked.

"When I was ten."

"Maybe you should try again," Drew said. "I ask my mom for an Xbox at least three times a year."

"How's that working for you?" Ruthie asked.

"It's not."

"So how is that good advice?"

"The point is, I'm still here. Nothing bad happened because I asked."

"I'd argue something bad has happened—loss of hope, along with, maybe, a lack of confidence in your negotiating skills," Sage offered.

"Nope," Drew said, meaning it. "I don't even want

an Xbox. My brother does, and he gives me five bucks every time I ask, so it's been kind of awesome. I'm two asks away from a new skate helmet."

Ruthie sighed. "Well, I'm probably a thousand asks away from a phone."

"Not if we present your parents with a cost-benefit analysis," Sage said.

"Or, like, we make a list of all the reasons why you would need it and show how it's worth the investment," Fonda suggested.

"Great idea!" Ruthie said, ignoring the fact that Fonda's idea *was* a cost-benefit analysis. Because the point was: her friends were united in a common cause, and *she* was that cause. "J'adore making lists."

Ruthie stood and dusted the sand off her legs.

"Where are you going?" Drew asked.

"To Circle K to buy a pen."

"Why?"

"So I can make my list."

All three girls flashed their phones.

"Oh, right." Ruthie sat. "Reason number one for needing a phone: no more pens."

They typed out that reason and came up with nine more. But the most important reason, the one that Ruthie didn't dare say out loud, was: when a girl finally has an even number of friends, she does not want to be the odd one out.

chapter four.

FACT: IN THE world of activism, the clothes you wear matter. And on Monday morning, fifteen minutes before the bell rang, Fonda went to Principal Bell's office looking like a girl who mattered. Her color palette was that of a woodland warrior: forest-green T-shirt dress, tan vegan-suede vest, leopard high-tops, and her beaded friendship bracelets, which she imagined represented the many causes she'd fought for over the years. And her hair? Side braids, of course.

The original plan was for Fonda to approach the principal flanked by Drew and Ruthie, who would also be dressed in woodland warrior chic. But Joan strongly disagreed. "Showing up to a negotiation with your best friends gives the impression that you're insecure," she told Fonda. "Every movement needs a face. And since you are the most passionate about changing the field trip, you, and you alone, should be that face."

When Fonda relayed her mother's theory to the girls, she expected a whole other kind of protest. One that accused her of stealing the spotlight or edging them out. Instead, she got hysterical laughter.

"I can't stop picturing a movement with your face on it," Drew said, wiping laughter tears from her eyes. "A *bowel* movement."

"Same, but it's not Fonda's face I'm seeing," Ruthie said. "It's the 'shocked' emoji's."

Fonda giggled. "Why the shocked emoji?"

"Because it's stuck to a bowel movement and it was *not* expecting that."

The visual had them cracking up all the way to the school. Which was another good reason to speak to Principal Bell alone. Because if the words *movement*, *face*, or *shock* came up during the conversation, the girls would lose it and Fonda's credibility as an activist would be shot.

So there she was. Waiting to check in with the office receptionist, breathing burnt coffee and eraser smells, her nerves rattled by the incessant hum of the Xerox machine and the ringing telephones. What made her think she could change a tradition? Make a difference? Fight for what she wanted, and *win*? Fonda was about to leave when she heard a familiar voice. "Pssst, how's my hair?"

It was Ava H. from the seventh-grade clique known as the Avas, because, well, when three best friends share the same first name, what else would you call them?

She was seated at a desk in the far corner of the office, microphone positioned under her glossy lips, ready to make the morning announcements. "Is it too frizzy?" she asked, petting her brown lob in steady strokes as if soothing an anxious cat.

Why was Ava H. even worried about frizz? Her hair was enviably reflective, and her announcements were broadcast to the school via loudspeaker, not camera.

Before Fonda could ask, Ava H. cut a look to the boy digging through the lost-and-found bin on the other side of the office. It was Henry Goode: permanently tanned, shaggy brown hair, devilish smile. He was Will Wilder's best friend and had a mini crush on Drew when school started. But Drew's crush arrows were clearly aimed at Will, so he nobly stepped aside. Did Ava H. know any of that? Hopefully not. Because her crush arrows were aimed at Henry, and her jealousy arrows were supposedly very sharp.

"Your hair is perfect," Fonda said. She was about to take their bonding further by complimenting Ava H. on her camouflage T-shirt and bronze leggings, because metallic was a bold choice for a Monday morning, but Principal Bell emerged from her office before she had a chance.

"Miss Miller," she said, addressing Fonda by her last name, as principals and angry teachers often do. Her bangs had split down the middle during her swift walk toward the receptionist desk. That, along with her long nose and thin face made her look like the picture of the Afghan show dog she wore on the lapel of her blazer. Something about that realization made Fonda relax a little. "How have you been?"

"I'm doing well, thanks. How are—"

"And those wonderful sisters of yours?" she asked. No shocker there. It was like Fonda was the salad and her siblings were the ranch dressing. People tolerated her to get the tasty stuff.

"They're fine."

"We miss them around here," Principal Bell said. "They kept things interesting, that's for sure."

Fonda's insides curled into fetal position and sobbed at the sound of that one. Joan often reminded her that a compliment directed at Winfrey and Amelia was not meant as an insult to Fonda. But, come on. When someone says "they kept things interesting," it implies that "things" are no longer "interesting" without them. "Things" that Fonda happened to be part of in that very moment. Unless, of course, she could make a compelling argument for Catalina Island and win. Maybe then Principal Bell would stop missing Winfrey and Amelia and start appreciating the Miller sister that was still there.

"I see you're on my schedule this morning," she said, suddenly all business. She indicated her office, offering Fonda privacy if she wanted it. But Fonda chose to plead her case in the open. Why not show Ava H., Henry Goode, and the receptionist that she, like her sisters, could keep things interesting too?

"Yeah, so speaking of Winfrey and Amelia," she began. "They went to Catalina Island over the Fourth and couldn't stop raving about how educational it was."

"Educational?" Principal Bell asked, head cocked, wondering where this was going. "What exactly did they learn there?"

Having anticipated this question, Fonda mentioned Catalina's renowned Marine Institute outdoor science school, astronomy hikes, beach amphitheater, nighttime snorkeling adventures, and the wild bison that had been imported to the island in 1924 for a silent film and never left. "As you can see, the opportunities for us to learn and bond are endless."

"It sounds wonderful," Principal Bell said in that grown-up way that Fonda found a little unnerving. Because how many times did Joan say "sounds wonderful" and then shut her down?

"I'm glad you agree, Principal Bell," Fonda said,

then smiled a little. After saying that name out loud, she decided that PrinciBell was more efficient. It would also make Drew and Ruthie laugh their ears off. "Which is why I propose we go there this year instead of Ferdink Farms."

Fonda shot a quick side-eyed glance at Ava H. to see if she had been listening. Ava H. flashed a thumbs-up to show that she was.

"I admire how well you articulated your idea, Ms. Miller," PrinciBell said. "But the students at Poplar Middle love Ferdink Farms."

Henry lifted his head from the lost-and-found bin. "Uh, no we don't."

"Like, not one bit," Ava H. added.

Fonda stood a teeny bit taller. Her movement had caught on faster than she anticipated.

"Hmmm." PrinciBell finger-combed her bangs into submission. "I can't imagine the rest of the student body feels the same."

Fonda glanced at Ava H., who urged her to go on. "They do. And I can prove it."

"How?"

"With a petition," Fonda said. With the help of Ava H. and Henry she could probably get the entire grade to sign by tomorrow.

"Interesting . . ." PrinciBell tap-tapped her dog pin. "What kind of educator would I be if I stood in the way of democracy?"

"Does that mean I can try?"

"Yes. If you can get one hundred signatures, I'll consider—"

"What about Camp Pendleton?" Henry said.

"The Marine Corps base?"

"Yeah. It's like thirty minutes from here, and it's awesome."

"More, uh, awesome, than Catalina?" PrinciBell asked.

Meanwhile, Fonda wanted to stuff Henry in the lost-and-found bin and seal it with a kick. How dare he hijack her plan?

"Way more awesome," he continued. "They have paintball and boot camp, and the beds are in real army barracks and—"

"And, *ew*," Ava H. said.

"What do you mean, *ew*?" Henry asked. "You're literally wearing camouflage."

"What does camouflage have to do with army barracks?"

Henry laughed, assuming Ava H. was joking. Ava H. blushed, because she definitely was not.

"The point is," Fonda pressed, "Ava and I think Catalina Island would be perfect—"

"Actually," Ava H. interrupted. "If we're going to change things up, I say we visit the set of *Makeover Magic*."

"Excuse me?" PrinciBell said, her patience starting to wear.

"You know that show where sad, boring-looking people get made over into happy, cool ones?"

"I don't," PrinciBell lied, because everyone knew that show. It was hosted by Lulu Green—supermodel, wellness advocate, and number twenty-four on the *Forbes* billionaire list. Either PrinciBell didn't have Wi-Fi or she was embarrassed.

"My aunty Jasmine is the producer and can give us a whole behind-the-scenes tour and introduce us to her experts. They could give us all makeovers and—"

"That sounds like a super-fun day trip," Fonda tried. "But for the overnight, I think Catalina would be—"

"Boring," Henry said. "Every guy in our grade wants to go to Camp Pendleton. I know that for a fact."

"And every girl wants to go to *Makeover Magic*."

"For the day, yes, but not overnight," Fonda said, aware of the frustrated quiver in her voice.

"We can make it an overnight if we want," Ava H. insisted. "You know, stay in hotels . . ."

Fonda turned to PrinciBell. Surely, she would put a stop to this nonsense. But no such luck. The woman exhaled so heavily her bangs split again. "I'm hearing there's a need to change things up this year, and I'm open to it, so I'm proposing—"

"Catalina Island?" Fonda asked.

"Camp Pendleton?"

"*Makeover Magic*?"

"A petition competition," PrinciBell said. "Whoever gets the most signatures by next Monday wins."

"Done!" Ava H. said.

"Easy," Henry said back.

"No problem," Fonda managed, even though competing against Ava H. and Henry was a very *big* problem—and losing in front of the entire school was going to be even bigger.

chapter five.

DREW WHIP-TURNED AWAY from the door of Fresh & Fruity at the first sight of Will. She couldn't let him think she was just sitting there, wagging her tail, waiting for him to arrive. Even though she had been. For like twenty-seven minutes.

Not that Will was late. He was actually right on time. It was that Drew, Fonda, and Ruthie arrived early to claim the big table before the eighth graders. And claim it they did—a victory that stopped feeling like a victory the moment Fonda saw who walked in next.

"He brought Hijack Henry?" she huffed, still bitter from their morning encounter. And who could blame

her. Henry commandeered Fonda's well-planned protest and drove it in another direction—one that could
get them pelted by paintball pellets and yelled at by a
thick-necked man named Sarge.

"Don't look," Drew insisted, trying to look bored—
as if meeting crushes at fro-yo shops was something
she did so often it bordered on mundane. Instead, she
turned her attention to this week's art installation—a
series of wall hangings made from plastic found on the
local beaches. But all the colorful twists and knots of
sea-worn forks, doll parts, and soda bottles couldn't
distract her from the fact that Will was about to spot
her, then walk toward her, then say hi. And then what?
What was she supposed to say after hi?

"Who's the girl?" Ruthie asked.

Drew lowered the rim of her green trucker hat and
sank into her chair.

"Keelie Foster," Fonda said. "A total bender if you
ask me."

"Bender?" Ruthie asked.

"Boy friender—a girl who's only friends with boys."

Ruthie giggled. "Did you just invent that?"

"Yeah." Fonda smiled for what may have been the first time all day. "You like?"

"Sounds like one of my mom's made-up words," Drew grumbled.

"Maters gonna mate," Ruthie said.

"Mater?"

"Mom hater."

They cracked up, which was perfectly timed. Let Will, Henry, and Keelie think they were happening upon a trio of carefree nesties who shared laughs and fro-yos after school—nesties who weren't bogged down with crush anxiety or petty jealousy. Nesties who probably forgot Will was even coming.

"Pen-del-tunnn!" Henry bellowed when he saw Fonda.

"More like Pen-del-DONE!" Fonda bellowed back.

A table of smoothie-sipping mom types began gathering their things the way mom types often did when middle schoolers showed up.

"Hey, Drew!" Will tilted his head toward the growing line of customers, a silent invitation for her to meet him by the yogurt dispensers. It was a power move for sure:

an indication that Will was comfortable taking control of boy-girl hang-out situations. It also made Drew's belly sink a little. All this confidence must have come from experience—experience with Keelie.

Now in line and standing awkwardly behind Will, Drew pretended to browse the flavors. Yes, pretended. Because anyone with a Fresh & Fruity coupon knew exactly what flavors they had. Still, she ogled those metal machines as if they might print out conversation topics or morph into relationship robots that offered nervous girls advice. Which they didn't. Instead, she and Will inched toward the toppings bar in cringey silence.

"What are those yellow things?" Will asked as Drew spooned her favorite topping onto a generous swirl of chocolate cream pie.

"Caramelized yuzu balls." She blushed.

A slow sunrise of a smile brightened Will's face. "Yuzu balls? I always thought that was tofu."

"Ew, who would put tofu on frozen yogurt?"

Will pointed at her.

"Look who's talking." Drew giggled. She placed her

cup on the scale and wondered if the cashier thought they looked cute together. "You added peanut M&M's and almonds to pecan praline?"

"So?"

"So, that's *nuts*."

"You're nuts," he said, the playful quality returning to his voice. It had been there when they talked in the past and vanished after the incident at Ava G.'s party. But it was coming back. Maybe that meant *they* were coming back too.

After handing his coupon to the cashier, Will made his way to the table. Rather than following him, like Keelie probably would have, Drew waited for Fonda and Ruthie. Did she do that because that's what good friends do? Yes. But she also wanted to make sure someone was sitting between her and Will. If she was too close, electricity might pass between them the way it had when they were falling in L at Ava G.'s, and her fro-yo would melt.

Not that it mattered. Henry sat on Will's left and Keelie gunned for the open seat on his right. Across from Keelie was the only available option. A reality made worse by the fact that she was eyeing Drew's trucker hat like an acquaintance she couldn't quite place.

"I used to have one like that," Keelie said, stirring her red concoction like a witch's brew.

Used to?

Drew saw her wearing it at the surf shop two days ago! That was why she bought one. Was she proud of being a copy*hat*? No. For one, she'd dipped into her skate helmet money to pay for it. And for two: pathetic much? She'd actually thought if she dressed more like Keelie, Will would L her more. But all it did was make Fonda ask if she had lice, or *Pediculus humanus capitis* as Ruthie (and scientists) called it.

"No!" Drew had insisted during their walk to school, in between classes, at lunchtime. They had been bugging her about it all day (pun intended).

"Then what's with the lice lid?" Fonda had pressed.

"I like it, that's all."

If Fonda was buying it then, she certainly wasn't buying it now. Her hot, knowing glare seared the side of Drew's cheek with a silent message: *I'm onto you, and the minute we're out of here, I'm going to lecture you on staying true to yourself and knowing your value.* That was the only problem with Drew's best friends: they knew her too well. When she didn't trust her own personality and tried to borrow someone else's, she got zapped.

"What happened to your hat?" Drew asked Keelie, mostly to avoid Fonda.

"I stopped wearing it," she said in that bored drawl of hers. "It made me look like a dude."

A flash of heat prickled the surface of Drew's skin. Fonda laugh-snorted—a sound she made when she was proven right but didn't want to brag.

Drew turned her attention to Henry, who was pinching tiny cups of yogurt into his mouth. "What's with all the yogurt samples?" she asked, casually removing her hat.

"Yogurt?" Henry paused. "Who eats *yogurt*?"

"Uh, all of us," Will said. "And so do you."

"No, I don't," Henry insisted, then sucked a dollop of pom raz from what had to be his tenth cup.

"What do you think *that* was?" Fonda asked.

"Yo."

Everyone laughed.

"And what's yo?"

"Ice cream," he said as if it should have been obvious.

"No, bonehead." Will laughed. "Yo is yogurt."

"*You're* yogurt," Henry said.

"Now that you've established that you like it, are you going to buy any?" Ruthie asked, miffed that he was violating the one-sample-per-customer rule.

"I can't. I lost my wallet on Saturday."

Will and Keelie exchanged a knowing smile.

Ruthie's blue eyes widened with concern. "Did you retrace your steps?"

Henry nodded. "I even checked the lost and found at school, even though I wasn't anywhere near school when I lost it."

Drew felt bad for Henry and a little disappointed in Will. It was one thing to play a practical joke, but it had been two days. The joke was over; now it was a crime. Or maybe she was disappointed that Will was more loyal to Keelie than to his best friend—that he was loyal to Keelie at all.

"What time is it?" Drew asked.

Ruthie consulted her pink cupcake watch. "Three fifty-eight."

"Here," she said, handing Henry her coupon. "You have two minutes to get a free medium. Hurry, before it expires."

Henry's dark eyes warmed. "Really?"

"Really," Drew said, happy to right Keelie's wrong ... until Fonda kicked the side of her calf.

Fonda's narrowing eyes asked, *Why are you helping my enemy?*

Drew raised her brows: *What am I supposed to do? Let him starve?*

Fonda cocked her head: *Yes, that's exactly what you're supposed to do. If you let him starve, he won't have the energy to compete in the petition competition and we can go to Catalina Island!*

"Hold up, Hank," Keelie called after Henry.

He stopped and turned.

She removed the checkered wallet from her army jacket and waved it. "Forgetting something?"

Henry hurried back to the table and dropped Drew's coupon like a bloody napkin. "Where did you find that?"

"Hanging out of your back pocket," Keelie boasted. "I told you you'd lose it."

He reached for it; she pulled it back. "Apologize."

You're making him apologize to you? Drew wanted to ask. But she didn't want Fonda to kick her again, so she kept her mouth shut. Not that it mattered in the end. Henry reached for the wallet and snatched it from Keelie's grip.

"Ha! Get wrecked!" he said, then hurried for the machines.

The moment he was out of earshot, Fonda leaned into the center of the table and said, "Does he seriously think anyone would pick Camp Pendleton over Catalina?"

"I would," Keelie said, twirling a strand of fuchsia hair around her finger. "The paintball park is rad. It's like being in a real video game."

"Or a war," Drew said.

"Yeah, it sounds kind of dangerous," Ruthie added.

"It's actually one of the safest sports in the world," Will said. "Statistically, there are less injuries in paintball than bowling."

"Probably because no one plays paintball," Drew said.

"Yeah, there's no way it's safer than bowling," Fonda said.

Henry returned, his yogurt buried under a kaleidoscope of toppings. "It is."

"Impossible."

"Possible."

"Imposs."

"Poss."

"Im."

"Po."

Without another word, Fonda slapped her phone into Ruthie's open palm. She unlocked it in seconds and started researching.

"She knows your password?" Henry asked.

"Yep," Fonda said proudly. It was 13 15 17—the nesties' house numbers. They used it for everything.

"I know yours," Will told Henry.

Henry smacked his phone into Will's open palm like a challenge. Seconds later, Will handed it back, unlocked.

"How did you know that?"

"We've been best friends since kindergarten. I know how your mind works."

"Do you know what I'm thinking now?" he asked, glancing first at his cup of yogurt, then at Will.

"Yes, and the answer is no. Get your own spoon."

"Dang." Henry pushed back his chair. "You're good."

"Bad news," Ruthie said, holding the phone up to Fonda's face. "According to a study by the National Injury Information Clearinghouse, paintball is safer than bowling. So is running."

"How is that even possible?" Fonda asked.

"You'll find out soon enough because I'm going to win the petition competition," Henry announced from the cutlery stand.

"You're not going to win!"

"Well, Ava H. won't, and you won't, and three minus two is . . . WON!"

"I already have fifteen signatures, not including parents. By tomorrow I'll have—"

"I have thirty-three," Henry said, pulling a crumpled sheet of paper from his pocket. "Not including everyone at this table."

"No one at this table is going to sign that, right?"

Drew and Ruthie nodded yes.

"Right," Keelie added.

"Really?"

"Really. Because Will and I already signed it."

"Paintball sounds kinda fun," Will said, as if apologizing to Drew.

"What about zip-lining, night snorkeling, hiking?" Ruthie tried.

"The makeover idea sounds better than that," Henry teased.

"Your brain needs a makeover," Fonda said.

"Your comebacks need a makeover."

"Your comebacks' comebacks need a makeover."

"Stop saying *comebacks*!" Drew shouted. "It doesn't sound like a word anymore."

"I know." Will smiled. "Same with *makeover*."

"Oh, so now you're siding with *her*?" Henry said.

"Siding? I'm not siding with anyone. I actually think you're going to win."

"Wrong!" Drew said. "Fonda is going to win."

"Bet?" Will said with a sweet half smile that told her this was not their fight.

"Sure," Drew said. "What are the terms?"

"Large fro-yo for the winner. Made the way we like them," Will said. "So yours will have tofu balls, and mine will have—"

"Nuts," Drew said, extending her right arm, excited to feel his hand. Which she did, but only for one unsatisfying second. Because the moment that electric current started to pass between them, Fonda yanked Drew away.

"Come on, we have signatures to get," she said, handing Drew and Ruthie their backpacks.

"No, you stay," Henry said. "*We're* leaving. Right, guys?"

Before long, both friend groups were racing each other to the door and charging down Mystic Avenue in opposite directions, each on a mission to destroy the other. It was a classic Romeo-and-Juliet moment. Two star-crossed crushes being pulled apart by dueling families. A story that didn't end well for Shakespeare's characters—and Drew was starting to understand why.

chapter six.

IN THE GOLDMAN family, any conversation worth its salt (an expression Ruthie never understood because if something was *that* good, why would it need salt?) began with a stroll into town for gelato and ended in tears. "Ruthie, Grandpa Stu had a heart attack . . . Ruthie, Grumpy Cat died . . . Ruthie, we're thinking of sending you to school in San Clemente . . ." But tonight's family conversation was going to be different.

Instead of suggesting they stroll to gelato, Ruthie invited them to dine on the back patio. Partly because she had fro-yo after school and too much dairy made her gassy, but mostly because she wanted the nesties nearby for moral support. And Fonda's bedroom window was right there. Let Fran and Steven think Ruthie prepared spaghetti Bolognese, set the table, and put sliced lemons in the water just because.

"How's everything going at school?" her mother asked, clearly sensing something was up. "Are you still enjoying the TAG program?"

Dr. Fran, a pediatrician, was still dressed in her navy-and-yellow seashell-print scrubs, which was not ideal. She was more relaxed once she changed into sweats. Still, Ruthie insisted her mother wait. If the Bolognese got cold, the meal would be ruined, and if the meal was ruined, Ruthie's parents might be irritated, and if they were irritated, they might not be receptive to—

"Wow, what's the occasion?" Steven asked as he opened the sliding glass door—tie loose, shirtsleeves rolled. "Isn't our anniversary in June?"

Fran locked eyes with her husband—a warning that something was up. "Ruthie did this. Isn't it great?"

He responded with a squint-nod. *I read you loud and clear.*

They had a twinlike telepathy that Ruthie found unnerving.

"So, how's school going?" he asked as he settled into his seat.

"Great," Ruthie said, amused. They obviously assumed this was about TAG. How cute. "We're growing a medicinal herb garden and learning to treat ailments with plants. Lavender is very calming."

"Noted," Fran said, chewing. "Thank you."

It was a polite *thank you*. Too polite. The kind of polite that reminded Ruthie of the blanket her mother draped over the couch to cover stains—a poorly disguised barrier to the truth.

"Great dinner, Ru-Ru," her father said. He lowered his fork into a mound of spaghetti and twirled. "When's the last time you surprised us with dinner? A few months ago, right? When you wanted a hamster?" His lawyer tie was loose, but his cross-examination game was tight.

Ruthie stabbed a meatball. "Don't remember."

Suddenly, a prism of light danced across the table. Fonda was sending a signal with her mother's compact mirror. She was getting impatient and wanted an update. Ruthie scratched the top of her head. Code for *Give me a minute*.

"Fun fact," Steven said. "I recently read that if you want something from someone else, beating around the bush instead of coming right out and asking for it reduces one's likelihood of getting it."

"Interesting," Fran said, even though it really wasn't. "Is that because stalling makes everyone nervous and—"

"Fine!" Ruthie said. "I want a smartphone."

Her parents exchanged another look. This one was dripping with concern. She hated when their eyes ganged up on her like that.

"Ru-Ru, you know how we feel about—"

"If I could have your attention, please . . ." Ruthie stood. A sign to Fonda and Drew that it was about to happen.

Another prism of light stuttered across the table; the nesties were wishing her luck.

Nerves rattling, Ruthie wished she had written her presentation on a piece of paper, if only to steady her shaking hands. But if she gave her parents reason to believe her photographic memory had been compromised, the only phone she'd ever touch would require a quarter, a glass booth, and a time machine. So she clasped her sweaty palms behind her back, cleared her throat, and began:

"According to some,

Smartphones make you dumb.

The irony is there,

Of that I'm aware.

But a girl like me,

Who uses words like *irony*,

Is wise enough to know

That a smartphone will help her grow.

I won't need a pen to record my thoughts,

Less plastic in landfills makes the planet less fraught.

I can access world news the moment it breaks,

Take photos of animals, forests, and lakes.

Track my location so you don't have to worry,

Send me a text, and I'll be home in a hurry.

I can download a book in seconds flat,

Search for pictures of Grumpy Cat.

Cyber savvy is essential these days,

I won't get a job without it, not one that pays.

I'll be responsible and charge it every night,

Oh, and did you know it comes with a flashlight?

I won't get addicted or post inappropriate pics,

I won't bully, or TikTok, or subscribe to Netflix.

Ruthie will still be Ruthie, I'll stay sweet as can be,

Just please let me experience the twenty-first century.

Thank you."

Ruthie breathed a gusty sigh of relief in anticipation of her parents' roaring applause. Instead, they stared at her blankly, as if Zooming on a screen that had frozen.

"What's wrong?" Ruthie asked, her legs weak from the uncertainty of it all.

"Wrong?" Her mother beamed. "Nothing is *wrong*. That was creative and informative and . . . it was fantastic!"

"Agreed." Steven chuckled. "I should start rhyming my closing arguments to the jury. It's incredibly compelling."

Ruthie casually scratched her shoulder, flashing the girls a thumbs-up. "Glad you liked it."

"We really did."

"Yes, it was very impressive."

Steven reached for the pitcher of ice water. Fran took a second helping of pasta. Were they seriously moving on?

"Um, so . . . what do you think?" Ruthie pressed. "Can I get one?"

Fran lifted her face to the setting sun, closed her

eyes, and smiled at something distant. "You remind me of myself when I was your age. . . ."

Ruthie shifted in her seat, sending another message to Fonda and Drew. *We're about to stroll down Memory Lane. Pack snacks. This is going to take a while.*

"I used to love this TV series called *Doctor Who*," her mother said. "And there was this one episode that featured a lava lamp . . ."

Ruthie politely covered her yawn. "I'm not seeing the connection."

"I wanted a lava lamp so badly I started doing all these chores around the house to prove I deserved it."

"Did it work?"

Fran grinned. "Well, I broke three china plates and accidentally mixed a load of whites with a red shirt and turned all of Grandpa Stu's golf clothes pink."

"Did you get the lava lamp?"

"Eventually. First I had to promise not to do any more chores." Fran laughed. "Then I had to get a job babysitting so I could save for it. Three months later, I got it."

"Nice," Ruthie tried. But, honestly? Old-timey

parent stories were kind of irrelevant. What did a wax-filled lamp have to do with a smartphone? Did it even have an alarm? "In case my poem wasn't clear, I'm kind of hoping to get a—"

Steven wiped the corners of his mouth with a napkin. "It was clear."

"It's a big responsibility," Fran said.

"I know, and I'm ready for it."

"Your screen time would be limited to one hour per day," Steven said.

"That's fine."

"We'd need to know your password."

"Easy. Thirteen, fifteen, seventeen—the nesties' house numbers."

"You'd have to stay off social media."

"No problem."

"We'd have to approve all your apps."

"What are apps?"

"You can't use it in the car."

"I would never. I'd rather look out the window."

"Or during meals."

"I'd rather talk."

Her parents exchanged another look. "I'm okay if you're okay," Fran said.

Steven nodded. He was okay too.

"Is that a yes?"

"Yes."

Ruthie pushed back her chair and began jumping up and down. Fonda and Drew started banging on the window. She had heard the Bible quote *Ask and you shall receive* dozens of times but had no idea how well it actually worked. "Can we buy it tomorrow after school?"

Fran stood and began stacking the dirty dishes. "That depends."

"On what?"

"How much is in your savings account."

"What savings account?"

"The one filled with all the money you're going to use to pay for it. Smartphones aren't cheap, you know. You also have to factor in monthly data and calling charges."

"But that's not fair."

"It's absolutely fair. I had to buy my own lava lamp."

"Mom, lava lamps were like a dollar. Phones are way more."

"Then you better find a good job," Steven said, standing. He kissed Ruthie on the forehead, grabbed a stack of plates, and followed his wife into the kitchen. "Great dinner," he called.

The conversation was over.

chapter seven.

IN THE LUNCH Garden, Fonda managed to speed-chew all eight pieces of her California roll before she and Drew arrived at their table. With only six days left to get more signatures than Henry and Ava H. (four if she didn't count weekends), slow dining was not an option. The petition-competition clock was ticking. There was work to be done.

Yesterday, after learning that Henry was in the lead with thirty-three signatures, Fonda and the girls had left Fresh & Fruity and run straight to the Gem House. If they were going to triumph over two of the most popular kids in seventh grade, they were going to need a plan. They were going to need an angle. They were going to need promotional bead bracelets.

"Let's start with her," Fonda said the moment Drew set down her tray. She was pointing at Toni Sorkin, a freckle-faced go-getter who had recently been named vice president of the student council.

"Hey, Toni," Fonda said, her smile leading the way. "I'm not interrupting anything, am I?" It was an awkward question since Toni was eating alone, but it was kinder than asking why she couldn't find a lunch buddy.

"Not yet," Toni chirped. "I'm saving the table for an emergency student council meeting, but it's not starting for another"—she checked her phone—"seven minutes. Why?" She flashed her palm. "Wait, don't tell me. You're miffed that the bike racks are being moved to the side entrance, aren't you? Well, you're not alone. That's what we're meeting about."

"Actually, we're fighting for a different cause."

As rehearsed, Drew gave Toni the clipboard and a pen. "Principal Bell said if we get enough signatures, she'd cancel the Slopover and let us go to Catalina Island. Will you sign?"

Toni's freckles lit up. "Totally!" She scribbled her name on the petition and handed the clipboard back with the can-do spirit that got her elected. "Last year's trip traumatized my nasal passages. I literally can't see a shovel without smelling horse poop. It's, like, a whole thing for me now."

"And what about the mattresses?" Fonda added. "Oily grandfather scalp, right?"

"If only . . ." Toni fanned the honeysuckle-scented air. "I think mine had been dipped in blue cheese."

Fonda and Toni shared a laugh while Drew procured the beaded *I ♥ CAT* bracelet. "We appreciate your support."

"Aw, thanks but no thanks." Toni politely handed it back. "I'm more of a dog person."

Fonda managed a patient grin. "Cat is short for Catalina Island."

"Oh, cute!" Toni took the bracelet back. "Henry didn't give me anything when I signed his petition. Neither did Ava."

"Wait." Fonda bristled. "You signed theirs too?"

"Why not?" Toni said. "I'll go wherever. As long as it's not Ferdink Farms, you know?"

"I do," Fonda said. But it wasn't that simple. If Toni

signed multiple petitions, her vote wouldn't count.

"Do you think everyone's doing that?" Fonda asked Drew as they walked away from Toni. Because if they were, she may as well rip up her petition and grab a poop-scented shovel.

Drew bit her bottom lip and shrugged. Her expression was the opposite of reassuring and enough to make Fonda scream. But Ruthie was now bounding toward them, and maybe, just maybe, she'd know what to do.

"I have six minutes," Ruthie said, bob swaying. "A compost specialist is coming to talk to us about sustainable—"

"Change of plans," Fonda interrupted. "We need to figure out who signed multiple petitions, then convince them to cross their name off Ava's and Henry's and stay on ours."

Ruthie opened her mouth. Fonda shook her head. This was not the time for questions.

"Are you open to financial incentives?" Ruthie asked anyway.

"Financial *what*?"

"Like, you pay me a dollar for every cross-off I get."

Fonda snickered. "Why would I do that?"

"I'm saving for a phone, remember?"

"Ruthie, if I had that kind of money, our bracelets would say *I heart Catalina Island* instead of *I heart Cat*."

"So, no?"

"I'll buy you ten phones if you get Keelie a full-time job at Ferdink Farms." Drew was glaring at her fuchsia-haired nemesis who was going table to table with Henry and Will, trolling for signatures. And the worst part? She was wearing that green trucker hat.

"How can you afford ten phones?" Ruthie asked.

"I can't. But if I could . . ."

Fonda closed her eyes and tried to collect herself. Yes, she wanted to dream up ways for Ruthie to earn money and help Drew overcome her Keelie insecurities, but right now? *Really?* If all three of their problems were patients in an emergency room, Fonda's would definitely be treated first. Ruthie's and Drew's problems were like broken bones, but her problem was bleeding out.

"Hey, girl," said Katharine Evans, an accomplished gymnast with an enthusiastic ponytail. "I heard you're giving out Cat bracelets, and since everyone calls me Kat, I was wondering if I could have one." She held out her wrist and cocked her head as if striking a pose for the judges.

"Actually, the *Cat* stands for *Catalina Island*," Fonda explained. "We want to go there instead of Ferdink Farms."

"I know, I heard," Kat said, wrist still extended. "That was your idea, right?"

"It was!" Fonda's sinking spirits perked back up. Finally, some recognition. "Are you interested in signing our petition?"

Kat lowered her arm. "What's with these petitions? I feel like I've been signing them all day."

"Yeah, but technically, you can only sign one, and it should be ours."

"What is Catalina again? A cat rescue shelter?"

Ruthie laughed, assuming Kat was joking.

"What's funny?"

"Nothing you said." Ruthie blushed. "I promise."

"Catalina is that island you see from the beach," Fonda explained. "It has snorkeling and hiking and zip-lining and ice cream shops and—"

"How would we get there?"

"Ferry boat," Ruthie said.

This time it was Kat who laughed. "Fairy boat? Really? Will there be magical wizards and unicorns too?" She rolled her eyes. "Now you're just making stuff up."

Fonda gave Drew and Ruthie a sharp look. *Let it go.*

"It's very real, and it's super fun," Drew said. "And it won't give you welts like paintball."

"Welts?" Kat said. "Owie!"

"Yeah, so you should cross your name off Henry's petition and sign ours. And tell your friends to do the same thing."

"Cool," Kat said, scribbling her name beside the number twenty. "Can I have a Cat bracelet now?"

After fastening the clasp, Kat hurried away to show it off. She didn't even *try* to remove her name from Henry's list.

"I better go," Ruthie said. "I've been gone for almost seven minutes. My teacher's gonna think I'm constipated."

"Wait!" Fonda pleaded. "This is a disaster. What are we going to do?"

"We'll figure it out after school, I promise."

But after school would be too late. Once Ava H. and Henry realized they couldn't have duplicate signatures, they'd start campaigning all over again and steal Fonda's votes. It didn't matter that Catalina was the best idea of the three. Unless Fonda could prove it, this was going to turn into a popularity contest—a contest she'd never win.

Drew slumped into an empty seat and unzipped her lunch box. "Now what?" she asked, totally unaware that she was sitting in the sixth-grade section.

Fonda sat beside her, too depressed to stress over optics. She had bigger political fish to fry. "How did the Women's March on Washington get its message to the masses? How do big movements do it?"

Drew giggled.

"What?"

"Doug had a big movement this morning. My hair almost fell out when I walked into the bathroom."

Fonda couldn't help but laugh. "Did it have a shocked-emoji face?"

"No, I did."

Normally, picturing Drew's expression in that moment would have cracked Fonda up. But there was nothing funny about a body full of welts or a face caked in makeover makeup. Not to mention the loss of pride. There was only one thing left to do: text Joan.

> Lots of competition. How do I get everyone to support Catalina? Protest, rally, or march?

> Start with a GIM.

> ???

> General Interest Meeting. Set up a time and place for people to come by and learn about your cause. If they believe in it, they'll support it. Make posters, post on social media, hand out flyers . . . gather as many people as possible. Talk more tonight. Love you.

Fonda put down her phone and turned to Drew, "We need to organize a GIM."

"Who's Jim?"

Fonda stood. "Our only shot at victory. Come on. We need to raid the art room."

"Jim's in the art room?" Drew asked, following her. "Is he cute? Maybe we can set him up with Keelie. You know, get her away from Will?"

"Sounds like a plan," Fonda said, thinking only of her general interest meeting and the slight bit of hope that still remained.

chapter eight.

THE FOLLOWING DAY, Drew was heading back to math class after a pee break when she heard, "Yo, D, what up?"

The voice was unmistakably Will's: deepish with a slight rasp. It was the D part she found so puzzling. Was it a term of endearment or a dropkick into the friend zone?

She finally turned, and there he was: blond hair spiked, denim-blue eyes smiling, red sneaks squeaking as he hurried to close the space between them. Drew's stomach dropped to the floor and did the worm.

"Hey, duh—" Drew paused midsyllable. She was about to call him W but thought better of it. For one, W didn't exactly roll off the tongue, and for two, if first initials *were* a friend-zone thing, she didn't want to encourage it. So she blurted "Dude," instead, which was worse. "What class are you escaping?"

"Science. You?"

"Math."

"Cool."

Drew nodded like a bobblehead while she searched for a quippy line or a charming observation to fill the silence. Something so fetching Will would fall in like with her all over again. But all she could muster was "So . . . Monday, right?"

"Yeah, things got kinda nuts toward the end."

Drew remembered the toppings on Will's yogurt. "Pun intended?"

He laughed a little, then quickly recovered. "We should do it again sometime. You know, like a do-over."

"Totally." Drew began bobbleheading all over again. Did he mean it, or was he just being polite? By "we" did he want everyone or just them? And if he did mean everyone, did that include Keelie? Drew made a mental note to search for a crush translator app when she got home. If one existed, she would download it twice.

"So what are you doing after school?" he asked.

Racing you to Green Gates so we can skate the bowl and talk about how much we L each other, Drew wanted to say. Instead she mumbled, "Making GIM signs with Fonda and Ruthie."

"Jim?"

Yeah, Jim. He's a pro-skater-slash-model-slash-musician who has a massive crush on me. The signs are to cheer him on because he's going to do an ollie over fifteen lions this weekend for a sponsored TikTok event, Drew also wanted to say. But only insecure girls lied to make boys jealous, and Drew wasn't insecure. Okay, fine, she was. And she would stay insecure until she knew if Will L'ed her more than Keelie. Still, she opted for the truth. "GIM stands for general interest meeting. Fonda is going to hold one tomorrow after school so she can tell everyone how cool Catalina is." The sparkle in Will's eyes dimmed a little. Assuming he was bored, Drew changed the subject. "What are you doing after school?"

"Skating with Henry, I guess."

Drew tried to look concerned. "What about Keelie?"

"She has band rehearsal on Wednesdays."

"Keelie's in the school band?" Drew asked, awash in relief. Not that there was anything wrong with band; it just wasn't one of Will's interests. And if band wasn't one if his interests, maybe Keelie wasn't one of his interests either.

"Not the school band, a garage band. They're called Roar, and Keelie is the lead singer. You should see them play. They're super rad."

Of course they are.

"Anyway." Will cut a look to the clock over the water fountain. "It's a bummer we can't all hang out later."

"Yeah, even if we weren't making GIM signs, there's no way Fonda's hanging out with Henry. Not after their fight on Monday," Drew said, hoping Will would suggest they hang without friends. He didn't.

"And Henry won't hang with Fonda either."

"I think they'd actually like each other if it weren't for this stupid competition. It's so annoying."

Will sighed. "I wish we were doing the class trip at your parents' camp. That place was cool."

Drew was touched by the compliment, but no way. For one, Battleflag was closed during the winter, and for two, she didn't want her parents tagging along on her seventh-grade overnight. "We can't all agree on one location as it is. Imagine throwing another into the mix."

"Solid point."

"Unless . . ." Drew tap-tapped her chin.

"Unless *what*?"

"Unless they called a truce."

Will raised an eyebrow. "They'll never do that."

"Well, what if we did it for them?"

"Like *The Parent Trap*?"

Drew wanted to hug him right there in the empty hallway. Not only did she and Will share movie love for *The Skateboard Kid*, he knew *The Parent Trap* too and wasn't afraid to admit it!

"Exactly like *The Parent Trap*, only without parents—"

"Or twins."

"Or Lindsay Lohan."

Will considered this for a moment. "So . . . how?"

"Hmmmm . . ." Drew scratched the back of her head. Unlike in the movie, she and Will weren't identical twins. They couldn't swap identities and trap their friends into making up. Or could they . . . "You know Henry's password, right?"

"Yeah."

"And I know Fonda's."

"Go on . . ."

"Get on Henry's phone after school, text an apology to Fonda, and say you want to be friends. Tell her you think Catalina would be fun, then delete it from Henry's phone. I'll send basically the same text to Henry from Fonda's phone and delete it. Then we'll lure them to Van's Pizza tomorrow at like five thirty. They'll think they've already made up, peace will prevail, and we'll have our do-over."

"This is way better than *The Parent Trap!*" Will beamed. "Text me when I should text you . . . I mean, when Henry should text you . . . I mean, when Henry should text Fonda . . . I mean . . . You know what I mean."

Drew giggled. "I will!"

"Okay, this is awesome," Will said as he hurried back to class.

"Thanks," Drew called. "You are too!"

Oops.

THE GIRLS HAD been in Fonda's kitchen for hours, making signs to promote tomorrow's general interest meeting, and the vinegary Magic-Marker smell was giving Drew a headache. Or maybe her mind was so stuffed with Will thoughts, they were jammed up against the sides of her brain.

Normally, Drew would have unloaded these thoughts on the girls, thereby ridding herself of the uncomfortable brain pressure. But she couldn't share details of the hallway hang, Will's knowledge of *The Parent Trap*, or her mortifying slip-up when they parted ways—not without revealing their devious scheme. A scheme that, if properly executed, would unite their friend groups and give Drew and Will a second chance at like. It was worth the headache.

"This GIM is gonna to be the jam," Drew said, eager to wrap things up so she and Will could set their plan into motion.

Fonda circled the kitchen table and evaluated. "Do you think fifteen puffy-paint posters and thirty-five flyers are enough to get the word out?"

"They will be if we throw in some free lollipops," Ruthie said.

"Where are we going to get lollipops?" Fonda asked. "I spent my entire budget on puffy paint."

"My mom's a pediatrician, remember?" Ruthie said. "She gives them to her patients to make them stop crying. We have hundreds of them in the garage."

Fonda gave Ruthie a gigantic thank-you hug. "I have a good feeling about this." She gathered a handful of her cinnamon-brown waves, then released them like a wish. "Once everyone learns how cool Catalina is, there's no way they'll support Ava or Henry." Her certitude was infectious. Her mood, calm and positive. It was time.

Drew sent a thumbs-up emoji to Will, and seconds later Fonda's phone dinged. Drew clenched her fists. She forgot to silence the ringer! Now Fonda would see the text and would respond to it herself—a response that Drew would not be able to control.

"Hand me my phone, please," Fonda said as she watched Ruthie paint a puffy heart on top of the *i* in *lollipop*.

Drew, having no choice, took Fonda's phone off

the countertop and entered the password. Maybe if she was fast enough, she could erase it and have Will send a new one. But Fonda was already standing behind Drew, reading over her shoulder.

"It's from Henry," she said, stunned.

Ruthie put down the paint. "Henry Goode?"

Drew nodded. "I wonder why he's texting you."

"Hopefully to let us know he's moving to Swahili," Fonda said, brown eyes shifting as she read the message.

"I think Swahili is a Bantu language used in East Africa, not a place," Ruthie said. And by *I think*, she meant *I'm 100 percent sure*. It was her way of politely correcting people without coming off as a know-it-all.

"And I think I'm hallucinating." Fonda showed them her screen. "Look."

> SORRY FOR BEING A JERK AT F&F. CATALINA SOUNDS COOL. TRUCE? VAN'S TOMORROW at 5:30? BRING YOUR FRIENDS.

"Wow!" Drew said a little too enthusiastically. "That's so nice of him. Let's do it."

"Do what? Walk into his trap?"

"Trap? Why do you think it's a *trap*?"

Fonda cocked her head. "Seriously?"

"Do you really think he's smart enough to plan a trap?" Ruthie said. "He didn't know the *yo* in *fro-yo* stood for yogurt."

"True," Fonda said.

"And pizza after the GIM would be fun," Drew added.

"Yeah, with you guys, not Henry." Fonda turned her attention back to Ruthie's puffy hearts.

Drew said, "Can I grab some popcorn from the pantry?" When Fonda said yes, Drew also grabbed Fonda's phone and texted:

> HEY IT'S FONDA. I'M OVER THIS COMPETITION AND SUPER OVER THE FIGHTING.
>
> CAMP P DOESN'T SOUND SO BAD. TRUCE? VAN'S TOMORROW @ 5:30 FOR A DO-OVER? BRING YOUR FRIENDS.

Drew quickly hit Send, then erased the text from

Fonda's phone. Moments later, Will texted to say that Henry bought it and was all in. Now all Drew had to do was convince Fonda to go to Van's after the GIM and everything between their friend groups would be good. Correction: everything would be *Goode*...

chapter nine.

"GOOD EVENING, MRS. Mumford," Ruthie said when her elderly neighbor answered the door. It wasn't even dinnertime, and the woman had already zipped herself into a flannel housecoat. She was clearly tucking in for the night, possibly the rest of the week, which made her an ideal prospect for Ruthie's new business venture. "How are you today, ma'am?"

Mrs. Mumford drew back her lips in amusement, revealing a crooked row of coffee-stained teeth. "Ruthie, I knew you when you were in your mama's belly. Please, call me Lorna."

"Thank you, Mrs. Mumford, I will."

"Wonderful," she tittered. "How can I help you, dear?"

"I'm starting a dog-walking service, and I'd love to count Balthazar among my growing list of clients. Does he still love chasing bunnies?"

"Oh, honey." Mrs. Mumford lowered her foggy blue eyes. "Zarzar passed six months ago."

"I'm so sorry to hear that," Ruthie said with a hand to her heart. Though she wasn't particularly fond of the gigantic poodle or his gigantic poops—which Mrs. Mumford never picked up off the sidewalk because of her sciatica—it was a serious bummer. "What about grandchild babysitting? I love kids, and I'm CPR certified."

"I should be so lucky. Both of my children are married to their careers." Her attention drifted to a mom pushing a baby stroller up the street. "If they did have kids, they probably wouldn't visit anyway."

Sadness weighed on Ruthie's body. She felt like she was talking to the Giving Tree. "Okay, well, thank you for your time," she said, tears pinching the backs of her eyes as she turned to leave. But what was making her cry? Mrs. Mumford's hopelessness or her own? "Oh, and just so you know, I can use my bike to run errands if you ever need anything from the store . . ."

"Are you saving for something special?"

"Yes," Ruthie said proudly. "A smartphone."

Mrs. Mumford clenched her jaw. "Those damn things are destroying your generation. If you ask me, you're better off without it," she said, then swiftly shut the door.

Eyes pooling, Ruthie crossed Mrs. Mumford's name off her list of possible employers. There was only one house left—the biggest one on the street. It belonged to Owen Lowell-Kline: the pick-me boy Fonda called Weird-O; the Girl Scout cookie buyer Ruthie would forever defend.

The home looked more like a museum of modern art than a typical neighborhood dwelling. All those sharp angles and glass panes made it impossible to imagine anyone eating buttery popcorn on the couch or lazing around in sweatpants. Did they even own sweatpants? Did they ever sweat? If the inside felt as cold as the outside, then no.

Ruthie rang the bell. Beethoven's "Für Elise" began to play.

"Coming, Ruthie!" Owen called.

"How did you know it was me?" she asked when he

opened the door. He was wearing red velvet slippers, socks pulled to his knees, khaki shorts, and a striped button-down; his dark hair had the neatly combed side part of a Lego figurine.

Owen wagged his cell phone. "Security cameras."

"Ah," Ruthie said, wondering what it must be like to have a cell phone that could see though walls. "Nice doorbell, by the way. Was that 'Für Elise'?"

He nodded. "Also known as 'Bagatelle Number Twenty-Five,'" he said with a shy smile.

Ruthie shy-smiled back. "I used to think it was about a girl named Elise who was covered in fur."

"Same!" Owen said. "I thought Beethoven composed the song to cheer her up. You know, because she looked like a primate."

Ruthie laughed. "Me too!" She appreciated that Owen said *composed* instead of *wrote*. Few people knew the difference.

"I like your hair, by the way." His full cheeks flushed red. "Short bangs remind me of Audrey Hepburn in *Breakfast at Tiffany's*."

Ruthie thanked him, though technically she was trying for the main character from the film *Amélie*. But she'd take it. It wasn't every day a boy her age mentioned her hair *and* a Hollywood screen legend in the same sentence. "Are your parents home?"

"No. They work late on Wednesdays." He chuckled. "Wait, what am I saying? They work late every night."

"Who takes care of you when they're gone?"

"I'll give you one clue," Owen said. "It speaks French and has two thumbs."

Ruthie squinted. She hated when she couldn't crack a brainteaser. "I give up. What speaks French and has two thumbs?"

Owen hitched his thumbs toward his chest. "Moi."

Ruthie giggled. Amused as she was, Owen's riddle also made her sad. Who did he talk to after school? Who did he eat dinner with every night? "Would you mind leaving a message for them?"

"My parents or my thumbs?"

Ruthie smiled. "Parents."

"Are you selling more Girl Scout cookies? Because I wouldn't mind giving the Lemon-Ups a try."

"No, I'm selling services this time. Dog walking, babysitting, chores . . . I'm saving for a phone."

"Hmmm," Owen said, glancing up at the orange-and-pink-streaked sky. "You're in the TAG program, aren't you?"

"I am," Ruthie said. "How'd you know?"

"We go to the same school, but I never see you around, so I assumed. Anyway, that means you're smart, right?"

"Smart is relative," Ruthie said. Her parents told her to say that so she wouldn't seem conceited. "But I get decent grades. Why?"

"I need a tutor."

"You do?" Ruthie asked, surprised. Why would Owen be a pick-me if he didn't know the answers? "What subject?"

"All subjects. I don't know how much you charge, but we can probably pay you thirty dollars an hour."

"You mean thirteen," Ruthie said, trying to look professional by concealing her elation. Because thirteen dollars an hour was almost three times as much as she'd make dog walking.

"No, I mean thirty. And I'll probably need help like four days a week."

"Seriously?"

Owen's chocolate-brown eyes held firm. "Seriously."

Ruthie didn't have to be talented or gifted to know that that would yield $120 per week. "I'll take it."

"Great!" Owen dropped his phone. Ruthie picked it up. "Can you start tomorrow after school?"

"I wish, but Fonda's hosting a general interest meeting about Catalina Island tomorrow. You should come. There will be free lollipops."

"Cool. I love GIMs," Owen said. "How about Friday, then?"

"Weekly sleepover," she said. "Monday?"

"Monday it is."

Beaming, Ruthie waved goodbye and ran home, fueled by the knowledge that she'd have enough money to buy a phone by Christmas and a protective case by New Year's. So what if Fonda thought he was a Weird-O; the pick-me picked her. She was officially employed.

chapter ten.

WHEN THE BELL rang, Fonda, Drew, and Ruthie blasted through the front doors of the school and positioned themselves under the flagpole to greet their audience. Soon, Catalina Island would be the new Slopover, the petition competition would be a thing of the past, and the nesties would be remembered as the trailblazers who rewrote field trip history.

Students spilled onto the front lawn, and Fonda lifted a bullhorn to her glossy lips.

"For those of you who don't know me, my name is Fonda Miller . . ." she began once the fifteenth person arrived. Fifteen, she decided, was the perfect number—big enough to start but not so big that the slow walkers would be too intimidated to join. "And I'm here to tell you about Catalina Island."

Leah Pellegrino, a DIY entrepreneur who sold pom-pom keychains and tie-dyed knee socks, raised her paint-stained hand. "Wait. Are you related to Amelia Miller?"

Fonda wanted to jam her bullhorn over Leah's head and make her wear it like a dog cone because only an animal could be that savagely rude. On the other hand, the crowd was thickening and Ava H. and Henry were probably halfway home, totally unaware that Fonda was stealing their votes, so why dwell?

"I am," she managed. "Now, back to Catalina—"

"What about *Winfrey* Miller?"

Fonda nodded. "Yep, her too. Now, back to—"

"I heard they went to the high school homecoming dance barefoot, so I started following them on Insta. And guess what?"

Fonda glared at her, refusing to guess.

"They followed me back! And guess what again? Amelia 'liked' my triple-pom keychain, so I named it the Amelia. You can tell her that if you want. I don't mind."

Fonda looked out at Drew and Ruthie, hoping for a supportive eye roll or a don't-let-her-get-you-down finger wag. But Ruthie was busy handing out lollipops and Drew was getting signatures, forcing Fonda to deal with Leah all on her own.

"You know what else Amelia likes?" she said, deciding to use Leah's pathetic obsession to her advantage. "Catalina. She and Winfrey partied there on the Fourth and said it was epic."

Leah and her friends exchanged delighted glances. Fonda, on the other hand, felt a bit ew. If the goal was to create a name for herself, *by* herself, involving her sisters was the opposite of that. Then again, this was a cutthroat competition. If victory required a bit of name-dropping, so be it.

"Do you want to know why Winfrey and Amelia said Catalina was epic?"

Everyone cheered.

"*C* stands for *clean cabins*. The mattresses smell like fabric softener. *A* stands for *activities*, because there are tons. Zip-lining, snorkeling, water trampolines . . . There's even a sea-life safari, a mini golf course, and night hiking."

A few of the boys *wooo-hoo*ed. She had this.

"*T* is for *travel time*, which is only an hour—by *ferry*! Goodbye, barfy bus rides, and hello, salty breezes. And the best part? There's a snack bar on board."

"Yay, fairies!" Kat Evans began flapping her hands like wings, still choosing to believe that a flock of magical creatures would lift them up by their shirtsleeves and fly them to the island.

"Dumb-dumb," Sage mouthed from the crowd.

Fonda tried her hardest not to smile.

"About the travel time . . ." Owen said as he smoothed his slick side part with the palm of his hand. "It's only fifteen minutes by helicopter."

"I know," Fonda lied. "But we'd need a fleet, and that's not in the budget this year." Ruthie and Drew gave her an enthusiastic thumbs-up—a sign that she handled him like a pro.

After a deep, centering breath, Fonda continued. "*A* is for *Avalon*, the town where we will buy ice cream and candy. *L* is for—"

"Look out!" a girl shouted.

Seconds later, something smashed against the back of Fonda's leg. "What the—" Red paint dripped down her calf, and the skin of a broken balloon lay by her sneaker.

"My bad!" Keelie called. "I was aiming for Dune!" Then, *smack*! A balloon broke against her arm. Laughing, she hurried over to one of the many metal buckets that had been placed on the lawn and grabbed more ammo. "You're so done, dude!" She drew back her arm and chucked a balloon at Dune's back. It exploded all over his gray hoodie.

Heart pounding, Fonda handed her note cards to Ruthie and marched straight onto the battlefield. "I'll be right back."

All around her, boys were dashing, throwing, and darting like boot-camp soldiers running drills. It was chaotic, it was childish, and it was seriously messing up her presentation. Fonda was right to think Henry's truce text was insincere. This was clearly some kind of Pendleton promotion—designed to pull a major Zeus and steal her thunder. "Keelie, what's going on?"

"We're just having a little fun."

"By throwing fake grenades filled with blood?"

"They're not grenades, Fanta, they're paintball-*oons*," Keelie said with a proud grin. "And it's not blood. It's—"

"Where's Henry?" Fonda interrupted. Because, so what? All she cared about was removing Henry and his band of war-hungry misfits from her territory before they destroyed her GIM.

"Knowing Hank, he's in the bushes, preparing to strike." Keelie scanned the perimeter. "All right, soldier. I'm going in." She removed her stained flannel shirt, tied it around her waist, and made a mad dash for the closest silver bucket. "Kamikaze!!!" she shouted as she ran into the hailstorm of balloons.

Chest tight and hands clenched, Fonda returned to the GIM to find Ruthie and Sage explaining how islands are formed to a much smaller crowd. Every boy had gone AWOL to join the paintball-oon battle, except Owen. His loafers were planted firmly on the lawn. Two lollipop sticks poked from his mouth like fangs.

Fonda, unsure of what to do next, stood off to the side, dabbing her watering eyes.

"Hey, at least the girls are still here," Drew tried.

"I guess."

"And that's how a volcano becomes an island," Ruthie concluded. After a dramatic curtsy, she handed the bullhorn back to Fonda while Owen generated a smattering of applause—applause that was barely audible over the battling balloon animals who had sabotaged her event.

"What's the point?" Fonda hissed. Dozens of plastic wrappers drifted across the grass—ghostly reminders of the boys who had crossed over to the other side.

"*We're* the point," Ruthie insisted. "If you're serious about saving us from the Slopover, you'll get back up there and fight for this. You'll fight for *us*."

Drew giggled. "Did you hear that last part in a movie trailer?"

"Yeah, it's rated M for Motivating. You should see it sometime," Ruthie said.

Then Sage added, "Go. They're waiting for you." She paused for dramatic effect. "We all are."

Ruthie and Sage were right—*they* were the point, and the point was: the threat of poop shovels, oily grandfather scalps, army barracks, and boring makeovers was very real; Fonda was their only hope. With that, she lifted the bullhorn to her mouth and with a renewed sense of purpose said, "As I was saying, *L* is for—"

"Lulu Green, everyone!" the Avas announced from the back seat of a golf cart as it turned into the student parking lot. Its surface was decorated with lip prints from hundreds of lipstick-covered kisses, and its headlights were adorned with flirty "carlashes."

"Hello, Poplar Middle School!" Lulu called over the blasting theme song of her hit show, *Makeover Magic*. "Are you ready to *be* the *u* in *beauty*?" she asked the stunned onlookers.

"That slogan is dumb," Sage said as her attention shifted to Lulu's driver—a tank-top-wearing Abercrombie ad with a well-oiled tan and roller-coaster arms. "He must be a bot, am I right? I mean, do humans actually look like that?"

"Apparently," Fonda said, having wondered the same thing about Lulu. The willowy limbs, the Barbie-blond hair, the brow-skimming bangs, the Granny-Smith-green eyes, and those teeth . . . Lulu's beauty was like a solar eclipse—too much brightness for the human retina to process. It hurt to stare, yet it was impossible to look away.

"Who wants an autograph?" Ava H. called as the Amber-bot drove onto the grass and turned off the engine. Girls hurried toward them like aliens returning to the mothership. Even the boys ran over. Within seconds, the golf cart was completely surrounded. Then Ava H. announced the catch. Lulu would gladly sign every arm, leg, sneaker, cell phone case, backpack, hat, hood, board, bat, and lunch box *after* Ava H. received an exclusive signature on her petition.

"Remember," Lulu said with a toss of her Barbie blondness, "all my products are edible and sustainab—"

Then *whack!* A balloon smashed against Lulu's arm. No one said a word. Not even Lulu. They just watched, shocked and silent, as red liquid spilled down her glitter-dusted skin and dripped onto her white cutoffs.

"Are you kidding me right now?" Ava H. shut off the music and stepped out of the cart. "Who threw that?"

"My bad," called a boy, his voice distant and small. It was Henry. He was on top of the school roof, palms splayed as if anticipating arrest. "Sorry," he said with a not-sorry smirk. "My aim sucks."

The Avas glared at him as if plotting to push him off. But not Fonda. She wanted to parkour up the side of the building and hug Henry full of thank-yous for what would probably send Lulu and her Amber-bot putt-putting back to Hollywood, never to return again. Maybe his truce text *was* sincere. Maybe he was trying to defend Catalina by chasing off the competition.

Lulu stepped out of the golf cart and raised her arm to the sky. "Is this solvent-based, latex, or oil?" she called.

"Cherry Kool-Aid and water," Henry answered.

"What kind of water? Tap, alkaline, or spring?"

"Brita."

Lulu exhaled sharply, then sauntered around the cart and stood in front of her driver. She offered him her arm, and without a word, he swiped a finger through the red liquid and lifted it to his tongue. After a moment, he nodded, confirming Henry's claim.

This time, Lulu's exhale was pure relief. "I thought it was toxic," she muttered, fanning her flushed cheeks. "I thought it was toxic!" she called to Henry.

"I would never do that!" he called back.

"I dare you to come down here and say that to my face!"

"Uh, okay."

The crowd made those annoying *oohhhh* sounds as if Lulu might grab him in her willowy embrace and make out with him or something. Instead, she gathered an armful of balloons and unleashed them on Henry the moment he was in range. Before long, a massive paintball-oon fight broke out on the lawn, which Ava H. managed to capture and post on her Instagram story. Every shot contained the supermodel in various states of amusement, with a caption that said *Lulu Green sees red. #MakeoverTakeover #PetitionCompetition #WeveGotThis.*

As Fonda stood on the sidelines, hate-glaring, she saw red too. Only her red was very much the toxic kind.

chapter eleven.

VAN'S PIZZA PARLOR smelled like dough, oregano, and angst. Drew knew it was the last place Fonda wanted to be after the slim GIM turnout—the first being a private place to sob herself snotty—but it was too late to back out. Will had managed to pull Henry away from paintball-ooning with the supermodel-slash-billionaire-slash-TV-star-slash-makeup-mogul and had texted to say they were on their way. Getting Fonda to a table should have been easy by comparison. Spoiler alert: it was not.

"What's the point?" she asked, refusing to step through the open door of the surf-themed restaurant, where tables were made of surfboards, autographed pictures of big wave riders covered the walls, contest videos played on a constant loop, and reggae filled the space with musical sunshine. "Pizza is for happy, successful people who didn't fail in front of their entire school."

Ruthie put her arm around Fonda and squeezed. "Not true. Unhappy failures eat pizza too. In the movies, sad people are always surrounded by pizza boxes. *Empty* pizza boxes. Which means they ate the pizza."

Drew laughed. Fonda might have too if she hadn't been shaking like a wet Chihuahua.

"I don't get it. Why can't Doug buy his own pizza?" she asked Drew for the third time. Thankfully, she was too distraught to remember Henry's "invitation"—the real reason they were there.

"His boss asked him to work a double shift, and he's starving," Drew said. Again. "I'll just run it over to the surf shop, then we'll go home. Unless you're hungry and want to stay for a bit. You know, since we're already here."

"Not hungry."

"Okay," Drew said. "Well, let's grab that booth in the back so I can order."

"Can't you get it from the counter?"

"Ankle," Drew said. "I must have twisted it skateboarding." She limped to the table and slid across the sticky red vinyl before anyone could object. "Ahhh, that's better."

Lying to her best friend—whose bottom lip was quivering—felt like a claw had reached inside Drew's belly and twisted her guts counterclockwise. Another gut twister was having to dip into her skate helmet savings fund and spend $5.99 on a slice of pizza Doug never asked for. But it was for a noble cause. One that went beyond Drew's crush on Will. This was about a social merger that would upgrade Fonda's status from "girl with friends" to "girl with a friend group that includes boys." And wasn't a status upgrade what Fonda always wanted?

"I'm glad we're sitting." Ruthie smiled. "I'm ravenous."

"Yay!" Drew's twisted insides unfurled. "What are you going to order?" Expecting outrage, she cut a look to Fonda, but her deadened brown eyes were fixed on the surf videos. She was that far gone.

"Tap water and free breadsticks," Ruthie said.

"That's it?"

"My phone isn't going to pay for itself."

"Please. You're gonna make bank tutoring Owen."

"I'll believe it when I spend it. Right now, the whole thing sounds too good to be true."

"I know what you mean," Drew said, wondering when Will was going to get there. If Keelie would be tagging along. If Fonda and Henry would realize they'd been set up and how angry they'd be once they did.

Just then, the bells above the door clanged and in they came. Cheeks flushed, clothes stained red, hair askew and sweaty, like extras from a war movie. To Drew, Will had never looked more adorable. Mostly because Keelie wasn't there to darken her view.

"How weird," Drew said, trying to project a convincing mix of shock and dread. "Look who just walked in."

Fonda stood. "I'm out."

"We haven't even ordered yet."

"You want an order? Here's one. Let's go!" She hooked her backpack over her shoulder and gave Ruthie a nudge, urging her to stand.

"Hey," Henry said to Fonda, his strides full of bounce and victory. "Lulu sent her driver to get more balloons, so the whole thing went on longer than I thought. Anyway, that's why I'm late. Sorry."

Afraid that Henry's apology might tip off Fonda, Will and Drew locked eyes, the intimacy of which sent a flutter of harp music to the spaces behind Drew's belly button. It was similar to the flutter Drew got from dropping into a bowl on her skateboard, only this one kept on going as Will sat down beside her. He smelled like cherry Kool-Aid, sunscreen, and *Keelie who?*

Oblivious to the fact that Fonda was standing, Henry slid into the booth and propped open a menu. "Thick crust with Hang-Ten toppings. Bam!"

"What did you mean, 'That's why I'm late'?" Fonda asked, still standing. "Late for what?"

Henry closed the menu. "This."

"This?"

"So . . . what was the deal with Lulu's driver?" Drew asked. "Was that guy even human?"

"Definitely not human," Will said. "He ran out of electricity halfway through the battle. Lulu had to plug the golf cart charger into his butt to revive him."

Everyone laughed, though Drew was the loudest.

"That sounds like some makeover magic right there," Fonda said.

"More like a make *under*," Henry added.

Drew offered her knuckles. "Good one, Goode!"

Henry fist-bumped her.

"Lulu's gonna need magic if she wants to get that Kool-Aid out of her hair," Ruthie said. "My friend Sage kooled her hair last month, and it's *still* pink."

"Kooled?" Drew asked.

"Yeah, that's what everyone in TAG calls it."

Henry smirked. "Kool."

This time it was Fonda who fist-bumped Henry, and Will and Drew exchanged another harp-flutter of a glance. Their instincts had been right; the "trap" was the only way Fonda and Henry would have realized their friendship potential. Sneaky as it was, it had to be done. In a few days, Drew would come clean and they'd all have a good laugh about it. Fonda would call Drew a social visionary, and Henry would insist they hang out together, like, all the time. Then they'd celebrate at Fresh & Fruity, where they'd toss around names for their new group like the Fresh & Fruity Five, the New Nesties, and DrRuFoHeWi, which would crack them up since it was so bad.

The waiter came, and Henry ordered an extra-large Hang-Ten for everyone to share. "My treat," he said when Ruthie balked at the price. "I heard the food sucks at Pendleton and you can't sneak stuff in because they check your bags. So when you're all hungry and mad at me, remember the pizza."

Fonda raised an eyebrow. "Pendleton? Why would we be at Pendleton?"

"The field trip?" he said, as if asking a question—a question he assumed she should have been able to answer.

Drew and Will exchanged another glance, only instead of a fluttering harp, it felt like that claw that twisted clockwise.

"We're going to Catalina for the field trip," Fonda said.

Henry scoffed. "Why would we do that?"

"Why *wouldn't* we?"

"Because Catalina is boring."

"Boring?" Fonda cut a look to Drew for backup. Drew lowered her eyes. "You literally said Catalina would be cool."

"I did not!"

"Did too!"

"When?"

"Yesterday!" Fonda unzipped her backpack. "Look . . ."

She was going to prove her point by showing him the text—the one Will sent pretending to be Henry, the one Drew erased.

The waiter returned with their pizza and an annoying amount of good cheer. "Any Parmesan for y'all?"

"No, thanks," Ruthie said after no one else bothered to answer.

"Pepper flakes?"

"No, thank you," Ruthie told him.

"Ranch?" he asked. "It's not just for salad anymore. You can dip—"

"All good!" Will snapped.

"Great, then," the waiter said with a clap of his hands. "Bon appétit, now you may eat!"

As he was leaving, Fonda muttered, "That's weird. The text is gone."

"Yeah, because it never existed!"

Will took a big bite of pizza and pretended not to notice Henry's frustration. A crumb of sausage clung to his upper lip. Drew pretended not to notice *that.*

"Can someone pass me a plate?" Ruthie asked.

No one did.

"I told you he was messing with me," Fonda told Drew. Then she dropped her phone in her backpack and zipped it with flourish.

"Me messing with *you*?" Henry tilted back his head and lowered a slice into his mouth. "How?"

"By calling a truce, then sabotaging my presentation with a third-grade balloon fight."

Henry drew back his head. "Third grade isn't water balloons—it's those toddler lollipops you gave out."

Will laughed, the sound of which made that claw in Drew's belly twist tighter. Whose side was he on?

"What's third grade about lollipops?" Drew asked.

"Yeah," Ruthie added. "Lollipops are timeless."

"No, Tootsie Pops are timeless," Henry said. "Those flat ovals are for baby teeth, and your presentation was, you know . . . Tell them, Will."

Will's cheeks reddened.

Fonda sat up a little taller. "Tell us what, Will?"

"Uh." Will shifted uncomfortably on the vinyl seat, which made a farting noise. Only the boys laughed.

"Tell us *what*, Will?" Drew pressed, though she wasn't sure she wanted to know. What if he said some-as tying with each other—and the prize, of course, which was boarding the van first so they could claim the front seats.

"Weekend plan alert!" Sage bellowed as they zig-zagged through the crowded school hallway, with its glass ceiling and sneaker-squeaking sounds. It was the only time TAG'ers interfaced with the regular students—the only time Ruthie felt like she fit into anything mainstream. "Sleepover at my house. We'll play Renaissance charades, watch the Michelle Obama doc, and spy on Steppy."

Steppy was Sage's nickname for her stepsister, Ava G. Spying on her was Sage's favorite, and only, form of exercise. Normally, it was low on Ruthie's list of favorite things to do, but what if the Avas got to talking about their campaign? And what if said talking led to some spilled strategy secrets? And what if said spilled strategy secrets helped Fonda outsmart Ava H. and win the petition competition?

"Weekend plan amendment alert!" Ruthie said as they pushed through the doors and into the blinding midday sun, where kids were arranging to meet at the

thing mean behind her back? What if he betrayed her?

"All I said was 'that GIM looks interesting.'"

Henry slapped a hand on the table. "What? No you didn't! You said, 'That GIM makes finals look fun.'"

Will cheeks reddened again. "I did not!"

"Then you said, 'Where would you rather go for the field trip? Rikers Island or Catalina Island?'"

Drew and Fonda looked to Ruthie for an explanation. "Rikers is New York's main prison. It's in the East River between Queens and the Bronx. It's supposed to be hell."

"You said that?" Drew asked.

"It was a joke."

"You're the joke," Fonda said, standing.

Normally, Drew would have tried to smooth things over, but she didn't feel like staying either. Will didn't have her back; he'd stabbed it, and she wanted to leave before he saw her pain.

"Where are you going?" Will asked as she stood.

"To get more wowwypops?" Henry teased.

"If anyone needs a wowwypop, it's you," Fonda said. "Because you suck!"

"Good one," Will said, offering to fist-bump Fonda.

As if that would make up for his backstab. It didn't. It made things worse.

It was obvious now that Will's loyalty lay with Henry, and that little piece of pork clinging to his lip wasn't helping. There was a time when Drew would have envied the pork for being close to Will's lips. But now she wanted to send it a thank-you note: *Better you on that lip than me,* it would read. Because she never wanted to be near Will's two-faced face again.

chapter twelve

RHEA, RUTHIE'S TAG teacher, struck the ancient sound bowl on her desk three times: the weekend had officially begun! Sort of. The Titans, as she called her students, were required to attend Saturday field trips, but those felt more like celebrations than obligations. They were *that* inspiring. And the best part? Rhea never straight-up told them where they were going. She gave them clues instead.

"Get a good night's sleep, everyone," she told them. "We're going on a real *mission* tomorrow."

"Mission San Juan Capistrano!" Ruthie and Sage shouted at the exact same time. The only thing more satisfying than beating their classmates to the answer

beach or the skate park, Fresh & Fruity or Van's. Ruthie's après-school vision, however, was far more intricate.

"I'm all ears." Sage adjusted her black glasses as if proving her commitment to listening.

"I have a standing sleepover commitment with Fonda and Drew every Friday, but tomorrow after the field trip, we can—"

Just then, someone came up behind Ruthie and covered her eyes with their hands.

She immediately felt the perpetrator's wrists: nine beaded friendship bracelets that smelled like Arm Candy—a delicious combination of vanilla-and-caramel-scented oils Fonda made at the Orange County Fair. Had the wrist only had one bracelet and smelled like coconut lotion with SPF, it would have been Drew's.

"What's up?" she asked, wiggling free.

"Nothing." Fonda sighed. "Everything is down." Her upbeat outfit—a polka-dot T-shirt, a floral skirt, and leopard-print high-tops—mocked her sadness like a birthday-party clown at a funeral. "Let's get out of here."

"What happened?"

Fonda, on the verge of tears, gazed out at the

parking lot, where students jumped into cars and mounted their bikes with a level of joie de vivre she seemed unable to fathom.

"Ava H. and Henry are tied with sixty-two signatures each," Drew explained. "So they're teaming up."

"For what?"

"A Camp Pendleton Makeover field trip."

Fonda sighed. "It's over."

"Ha!" Sage shouted. Several people turned around and gave her the stink eye.

Ruthie's cheeks burned. So much for fitting in.

Sage waved them off like a swarm of poop-shovel flies, linked her arm through Fonda's, and said, "A Camp Pendleton Makeover field trip is the second-dumbest idea I've ever heard."

"What's the first?" Fonda dared.

"You saying it's over."

Ruthie felt a zing of gratitude. She loved her pink-haired friend, now more than ever. Fonda needed a tough-love speech about perseverance and grit, and Sage was the only one brave enough to deliver it.

"But it *is* over," Fonda pressed.

"Only if you're a pathetic quitter who would rather plan a pity party than an effective strategy to crush the competition," Sage declared. "And if you are, tell me now, because I'll let go of your arm immediately so no one thinks we're friends. I do have a reputation to maintain."

Drew and Ruthie exchanged a delighted glance.

"What reputation is that?" Fonda asked.

"As a keen political strategist who has put five class presidents in office."

"Yeah, but this is bigger than a class election. This is—"

Sage dropped Fonda's arm and turned to Ruthie. "So about sleeping over—"

"Wait!" Fonda pleaded. "I won't be a pathetic quitter. I'll listen."

"There's just one problem," Sage said. "You already have sleepover plans, which is a shame because the Avas are sleeping over and we could spy—"

"Wait!" Fonda said, brightening. "Let's move the sleepover to your house!"

"So you, Drew, and Ruthie would come to my

house?" Sage nod-pouted slowly, as if considering this for the first time. "Hmmmm . . . I mean, two TAGs *are* better than one . . ."

"Let's do it!" Ruthie said, imagining the game of Renaissance charades they would play when the planning meeting was over. "Drew?"

"Sounds good to me," she said, blond ponytail wagging in agreement.

"Okay, then." Sage glimpsed her gold high-tops to downplay her excitement. She did it every time she got a compliment from Rhea or a perfect grade, which was *always*. "You guys go home and pack. I'll pick up my bike and ride back, and then we'll go into town for snacks."

Their moods, like Fonda's outfit, could not have been brighter. But no one was more excited than Ruthie, who would have all her friends at one sleepover.

Teeming with hope, the girls ran down the street, shouting out items they needed to pack.

"There you are!" Owen panted as he jogged toward Ruthie. "I've been looking everywhere. You really need a phone."

Ruthie stopped running. "Highly aware. What's up?"

"I have a bio test on Monday."

"Nice," Ruthie said, picking up her pace. Those snacks weren't going to buy themselves.

"And I need your help A-SAP."

"Oh," Ruthie said. "Well . . . I have a field trip tomorrow, but I can come on Sunday."

"No can do. I need help tonight."

The zing fizzled. "I can't tonight, Owen. I'm sorry. But Sunday—"

He shook his head. His Lego hair didn't move. "I really need help while the lesson is still fresh in my mind . . ."

Ruthie tried to process. "Uh . . ."

"If you can't do it, it's okay," Owen said, cheeks red and blotchy. "My mom found another tutor who wants the job. But if you can do it, we'll pay you double, you know, on account of the short notice."

"Double?"

"Duh-ble." He held up two fingers.

"Okay," Ruthie said as she watched Fonda and Drew disappear into their houses. Did they even notice she was gone? "I just have to tell my mom. I'll be over soon."

"Thanks, Ruthie. You're a lifesaver."

And you're a life killer, Ruthie wanted to say back. Instead, she thanked her new boss for the opportunity and told herself that the sacrifice would be well worth it in the end. Hopefully, she'd be right.

chapter thirteen.

"*THIS* IS YOUR room?" Fonda asked Sage because, come on! Black walls, drawn curtains, and rock posters were not typical TAG. Where were the bookshelves stuffed with five-thousand-piece puzzles? The literary classics? The academic achievement awards? Where were the spinning globes? The inspirational quotes? The solar system mobiles? The ceramic owls?

Sage tapped an app on her phone. Strings of fuchsia LED lights popped on. "Not what you expected?"

"Uh . . ." Fonda didn't want to seem judgy, but this was not the bedroom of an intellectual snob; it was a clubhouse for bats. "I just—"

"Are you flippin' kidding me right now?" Drew

blurted. She was standing in front of the posters, each featuring a leather-clad, pink-haired, wide-mouthed singer who gripped the microphone like a starving woman clinging to her last baguette. "*You* like Inga Thornbird?"

"I do." Sage sat on her bed and reached for the electric guitar she had propped up against the headboard. She began fingering the strings with the ease of a skilled musician.

"My brother is obsessed with her," Drew said. "He even thinks she's hot. Which is weird, because she's, like, old."

"Same with my sisters," Fonda said. "They dressed up as Inga for Halloween a few years ago."

"Old?" Sage looked down at her strings. "She was thirty-three when she died."

"No way," Fonda said. Not so much because Inga died young, but because Sage knew her age when it happened. "I didn't realize you were such a superfan. I thought you wore all-black because of the whole Steve-Jobs-did-it-so-he-wouldn't-waste-creative-energy-thinking-about-clothes and you wanted to be like Steve."

"That *is* why."

"And I thought your hair was pink because you kooled it and now you can't un-kool it."

"Affirmative," Sage said.

"And aren't you super into jazz music?"

The LED lights automatically switched from fuchsia to yellow.

"Jazz is my favorite," Sage said. "Why?"

Fonda indicated the posters. "Then what's all this?"

Sage set down her guitar. "My mom."

Fonda laughed. There was no way! "That explains the guitar."

"No, it doesn't," Sage said. "My mom was a singer-songwriter, dumb-dumb. The ax is all me."

"Wait," Drew said. "Inga Thornbird is really your mom?"

"Was. She died in a car accident when I was two. The press was too much for my dad, so we left Los Angeles and moved here to hide out. Steppy has no idea, and we need to keep it that way. Understood?" Her tone was serious, and her eye contact was strong.

"Understood," the girls answered.

"Good," Sage said, satisfied. "Moving on. Now tell me why I should vote for Catalina Island."

"Well . . . um . . ." The sudden gear change threw Fonda. Who *was* this girl? Not that it mattered. Sage's unpredictable personality held Fonda's attention the way Inga held that mic. No wonder Ruthie liked her so much.

"Tell me," Sage insisted. She was standing in front of the empty black wall, holding a piece of chalk.

"Well, I think it'll be fun and—"

"Borrrr-inggg!"

Laughing, Drew buried her face in the grocery bag and unpacked their snacks.

"Your campaign is missing three crucial ingredients," Sage began. "Strategy, strategy, and strategy." She wrote *Catalina Sea Monster* on the black wall and underlined it twice. "On Monday, Ruthie and I will start a rumor about an elusive sea creature named Pearl, who only shows herself two days a year—the same two days as our field trip. Curiosities will be piqued, and cameras will be ready, especially when we tell them that the *Catalina Times* pays for Pearl pics." Next, Sage wrote *Makeover Takeover*.

"What's that?"

Sage pointed at the open laptop on her desk. "I was head of the yearbook committee last year—totally unprecedented for a sixth grader, by the way. But the point is, I have all the student photos on my computer." She removed her glasses. "Even the bad ones."

Drew and Fonda glanced at each other. Where was she going with this?

"Everyone had five pictures taken, and we printed the best one," Sage clarified. "Which means I have the worst ones. I propose we print them out, write a bunch of desperate letters from desperate girls who desperately need makeovers, and get them to Lulu ASAP. Then, *bcchhh*." Sage splayed her fingers, miming a full-on head explosion. "Instant overwhelm. And if I know Lulu, she'd rather shut the whole thing down than leave someone out."

"You know Lulu?"

"I read her memoir," Sage said, surprising Fonda yet again. "Next, we get your sisters to post pictures of them having fun in Catalina."

"Ha!" As if Winfrey and Amelia would ever help. "The last time they did anything for me was never," Fonda said.

"That's about to change." Sage disappeared inside her closet and emerged with two signed Inga Thornbird posters, two Inga Thornbird tank tops, and two Inga Thornbird leather tassel keychains. "These should sweeten the deal."

"Genius!" Fonda said.

"No, the real genius is this . . ." Sage wrote $62 + 62 + 11 = 135$.

"How is that genius?" Drew asked.

"Those are the number of signatures on each petition. Henry and the Avas have sixty-two each, and Fonda has eleven."

Fonda's stomach dipped. It sounded even more pathetic when spoken aloud.

"That brings the total number of voters to one hundred and thirty-five. But there are one hundred and ninety-eight students in seventh grade. That means sixty-three were too lazy to vote. Any guesses as to who the sixty-three are?"

"Surfers," Drew and Fonda said together.

"Exactly! Drew, your brother surfs, am I right?"

"Every morning."

"Perfect. Hit the beach with him tomorrow. Take a fresh petition, a basket full of snacks, and a winning attitude. Paddle out. Harpoon them. Catch them in a lobster net if you have to. Just get those signatures."

"She will," Fonda said proudly. "Drew could teach a master class on scheming."

"I could?"

Fonda shook an imaginary Magic 8 Ball. "All signs point to yes."

Drew bit down on her thumbnail. "Why would you say that?"

"Why wouldn't I?"

"Why *would* you?"

"I think you know the answer to that," Fonda said with a slight wink. She was trying to remind Drew of the time she snuck onto Doug's computer, wrote an apology email to their mom, and signed his name. They had been in a fight, and Doug refused to apologize. So Drew, in the name of family peace, did it for him. If Drew hadn't sworn Fonda to secrecy, she would have reminded her out loud. But for now, winks were her best option.

"I'm so sorry." Drew sat on Sage's bed and lowered her head into her hands. "How did you figure it out?"

"Um, you told me?"

"When?"

"Like two minutes after you sent the email to your mom."

Drew lifted her face. "My *mom*? Wait, you're talking about the apology I wrote for Doug?"

"Yeah. Why? What were you talking about?"

"Ugh." Drew buried her face in her hands again. "Not that."

Fonda lifted Drew's chin and glared into those squinty hazel eyes of hers. "Then *what*?"

"The text Henry-slash-Will sent you and the one you-slash-me sent back to Henry."

"I-slash-you sent a text to Henry?"

Drew winced. "We did."

"About what?"

"Meeting at Van's."

Fonda felt the sharp punch of clarity right between her ribs. "No wonder I couldn't find the text from Henry. You erased it!"

"I just wanted everyone to get along."

"Yeah, so you and Will could hang out!" Fonda snapped. "You played me."

"I didn't play you!" Drew stood. "I mean, yes, I wanted everyone to get along so Will and I could hang out, and I knew you'd never form a truce with Henry on your own, so I schemed a little—"

"A little?"

"But when they started ganging up on you at Van's, I left. I chose *you*."

Fonda wanted to argue back, but Drew was right. In the end, she chose Fonda. And wasn't that what mattered? "Still, did you have to be so sneaky?"

"Yes, Fonda! Yes, she did!" Sage pulled them both into a hug. "It proves Drew's cut out for politics. And we know I am because I made up the story about the Avas sleeping over here so you'd come—"

"You made that up?"

"I did, and you're welcome," Sage said. "But the real question is: are you cut out for politics?"

"Since when is politics about lying to get what you want?"

"Since the earliest hominid of primitive bipedalism arose some six to seven million years ago," Sage said. "That said, I prefer the term *strategizing* to *lying*. Now, can you handle it or not?" She offered her right hand for a shake.

Having decided that "strategizing" was better than losing, Fonda shook it. "I *am* the hand in *handle it*."

chapter fourteen.

DREW CALLED DOUG from the sleepover to tell him the plan.

"A basket full of snacks?" He laughed. "Who came up with *that*? Little Red Riding Hood? What you need is an insulated backpack full of bean-and-cheese burritos."

"How am I supposed to get all that by tomorrow morning?"

"Get up at four a.m., bike home from Sage's, and bust out a bunch of bean 'n' cheesers. I'll provide the pack free of charge. Just make sure you're in the truck by five thirty a.m. A south swell is coming, and the lineup is gonna be jammed with shubies. Dawn patrol is a must, and I will wait for no one."

"Got it," Drew said, even though most of what he said made zero sense.

✕

THE NEXT MORNING, Drew was, however, very much on time. The damp chill inside Doug's truck and the pre-dawn darkness proved it. As did his annoyingly loud yawns.

Doug cracked a window. "It smells like farts in here."

"It's the bean 'n' cheesers," Drew told him, eyes dry and burning. Making stacks of burritos before sunrise was exhausting. How did Taco Bell do it?

"Yesss!" Doug reached for the backpack. "I'm starving!"

Drew slapped his wrist. "Watch the road."

"Grab a couple for me, will ya?"

"They're for the surfers."

"I'm a surfer!"

"Well, you don't qualify to sign my petition, so you don't qualify for a burrito."

"Good," Doug said. "They smell like farts anyway."

"You're the one that wants one, fart eater."

"You're the one who made them, fart cooker."

They rode the rest of the way in sleepy silence. As the charcoal-dark sky brightened into a more hopeful shade of blue, Drew was reminded of Will's denim-colored eyes. Like actual denim, they could be soft and comfy or rigid and tight—something to slip into or a fit that had to be forced. When they parted ways at Van's, divided once again, Drew had been sure Will's brand of denim was the bad-fit kind. But that was two days ago. Now there was a swirling fall wind where her anger used to be. It felt like hunger without the appetite, a pit that food couldn't fill.

Within minutes of arriving at Salt Cove, Doug was fist-bumping his buddies and saying, "Sup, bruh?" in that deep, monosyllabic bro voice that made Drew's cringes cringe. This from a guy who sang Taylor Swift songs in the shower and plucked his unibrow. If they only knew . . .

"What smells like farts?" asked Doug's buddy TJ.

"My sister."

With that, Drew hurried toward the beach, where neoprene-clad surfers ambled toward the frothing ocean, leaving traces of coconut-scented sunscreen in their wakes. Tanned and fit as they were, Drew only had eyes for seventh graders and eventually found them waxing their boards by the shoreline. They looked like a pod of seals in their black wet suits—hungry seals, she hoped. "Who wants a burrito?"

Everyone raised their hands. This was going to be even easier than she thought.

"You all go to Poplar Middle, right?"

They nodded.

"Great, so, um, for those of you who don't know me, my name is Drew, and I'm working to change this year's field trip from Ferdink Farms to Catalina Island, which you're going to love because—"

"Where are the burritos?" asked a boy with stripes of orange zinc on his cheeks.

"Sign my petition to show you support the change, and I'll give you one." A wave crashed on the shore and sprayed Drew salty. She ignored it like a pro and kept right on talking. "Who wants to go first?"

"Me!" Orange Stripes called as a line quickly formed behind him.

Drew handed him the clipboard and then a burrito. "You won't regret it. Catalina is an island, so we'll be surrounded by waves. Remember to bring your boards because the surf will be epic."

"Fake news!" shouted a familiar voice. It was slightly nasal and wildly unwelcome because it was walking toward them with Will.

"What are you doing here?" Drew asked Keelie.

She stuck her yellow surfboard in the sand with the flourish of an astronaut on a moon landing. "What do you *think* I'm doing here?" She pulled a clipboard and a pen out of her backpack, to be extra clear.

Another wave crashed, splattering them with spray. Unlike Keelie, who was dressed in a formfitting Hawaiian-print rash guard, Drew was rocking pajama bottoms and crusted zit cream. Still, she stood tall and took the ocean's sloppy licks like a splash-zone champ. Weakness was not an option.

"Hey, D." Will waved as if everything between them was perfectly normal. Which it absolutely wasn't. Not only did he call her D (again!), but he'd never apologized for comparing Catalina to Rikers. Since their encounter at Van's, removing the sausage from his lip was the only thing Will had done right.

"Did you come to steal my signatures?"

"Steal? Please! We had no idea you'd be here." Keelie shielded her eyes from the morning glare. "Your skin is so pale it's, like, invisible. I thought you hated the beach."

"I love the beach!" Drew said, mad at herself for taking the bait. "Anyway, I'm kind of in the middle of something, so if you wouldn't mind—"

"The only thing you're in the middle of is lying," Keelie said. "According to Willy, the decent breaks on Catalina Island are impossible to reach without a boat."

Willy?

"Dude." The boy who was about to sign the petition lifted his pen off the page. "Is that true?"

Will gazed out at the shore pound and nodded.

"They're just messing with you," Drew said, hoping Will would take it back.

He didn't.

"The good news is," Keelie chirped, "San Onofre, also known as the Waikiki of Cali, is super close to Camp Pendleton, so if you'd rather surf there, sign *our* petition."

"Rad!" The boy handed back Drew's clipboard. Only three people had signed.

"Can we still grab one of those burritos?"

"Is that what I smell?" Keelie asked. "I thought Drew pooped her pj's."

Drew hooked the backpack over her shoulder while everyone laughed, everyone except Will. He stood on the edge of their cluster, nibbling his thumbnail and watching the waves. His eyebrows knit with concern, maybe even guilt. Though not enough to defend her.

Fighting tears, Drew hurried for the parking lot, wondering how she'd face the girls after this colossal failure.

"What's wrong?" Doug called as she ran past him and his friends.

"Everything." Drew released the backpack to the sand. "You can have them."

His buddies descended on them like seagulls.

"Did you get your signatures?"

Drew shook her head. "It's over. There are no good surf spots on Catalina. I mean, there are, but you need a boat."

"There's Shark Harbor."

"Is it infested with sharks?"

"Nah. They call it Shark Harbor because there's a

rock by the break that looks like a shark head. It's a medium-sized wave, but it's powerful."

"Lower your voice, bruh," TJ said. "That break is sacred. I don't want a bunch of seventh-grade groms out there."

"Whatever," Drew sighed. "It's too late anyway. Keelie and Will probably have everyone's signatures by now. Catalina's over."

A girl screamed. It was Keelie. Clipboard in hand, she was attempting to outrun a gigantic wave but only made it a few steps before a claw of thundering white-wash smacked her flat. Most people covered their mouths in horror, but a few captured the glorious wipe-out on their phones.

Shocked and wobbling, she emerged like some sort of water zombie, arms stiff and dripping in seaweed. "Find the clipboard!" Keelie shouted at Will just as another wave smacked her back down.

When Keelie popped up again, she and Will began searching the ocean for their lost signatures. Drew, however, began searching her inner strategist for a way to capitalize on the "unfortunate" situation.

"Has anyone heard of the secret surf spot called

Shark Harbor?" she asked the boys. Ten minutes later, she had seventeen more signatures. And ten minutes after that, she was laughing herself breathless at the video someone posted on @Kookslams of Keelie getting pummeled.

chapter fifteen.

RUTHIE PRESSED THE Lowell-Klines' doorbell with the kind of determination that turns fingertips white. Friday's tutoring session had been a mild disaster, and she refused to let Owen's toddler-sized attention span, spontaneous snack cravings, and restless leg syndrome get the better of her again. Not only had she missed the sleepover strategy meeting with Sage, but she and Owen were only able to cover one-tenth of the material. And now it was Sunday. His biology test was less than twenty-four hours away. If Owen didn't focus, he was going to fail. And if the student failed, the teacher failed too.

As "Für Elise" sounded throughout the house, Ruthie rolled back her shoulders, lifted her chin, and deadened her eyes. She wanted to project an air of seriousness. Today, Owen would treat her like a professional whether he liked it or—

The front door swung open, and Owen thrust two helmets at Ruthie. "Hold these for a second." He wiggled a backpack onto his shoulders, shouted goodbye to his mother, then said, "To the garage, m'lady!"

"The garage? Why? What's happening?"

"It's seventy-six degrees and sunny. That's what's happening." The coarse fabric on his beige shorts made a scraping sound as he led the way.

"What does the weather have to do with cells?" Ruthie asked, steering his attention back to biology.

"Staying inside feels like being in a cell. That's what."

Ruthie smiled a little. It was a clever response, she had to give him that. But her laissez-faire attitude stopped the moment Owen wheeled an electric bike toward her and pat-patted the seat. "Helmet up and hop on. We're riding this steed to Dana Point Harbor."

"No, we're not!" Ruthie pulled a stack of flash cards from the back pocket of her overall shorts. "We're studying."

"At the harbor." Owen slid on a pair of blue mirrored

sunglasses. "My mom is hosting a lunch for her book club." He checked his Apple Watch. "In ten minutes, our entire neighborhood is going to reek of Le Labo perfume and Teslas. Trust me. We should get going."

Owen steadied the bike so Ruthie could get on. Was she thrilled about the location change or the idea of wrapping her arms around Owen? Not one bit. But the boat-filled harbor was the whale-watching capital of the west.

"Hold on tight," Owen called. "Here we go!" He thumbed the throttle, and they lurched forward.

"Ahhhh!" Ruthie grabbed Owen's hips and turned her face to the side—anything to avoid inhaling his skin smells, which she assumed were yeasty and sweaty and a lot like kombucha.

When they reached a steady cruising speed, Ruthie unclasped her hands and hooked her fingers through his belt loops instead. In the movies, when boys and girls doubled on bikes, they usually ended up falling in love. And Ruthie didn't want to leave any room for mis-understandings. Not that Owen was testing positive for the crush virus. He wasn't. But just in case . . . Ruthie shook her head. Even thinking about it was awkward.

"Told you we should get outside," Owen called into the salty breeze.

He was right. The postcard perfection of the day was undeniable. Sunshine colored the neighborhood streets in yellow joy, and everyone smile-waved when they cruised by. And the best part? Owen's skin didn't smell of kombucha, more like expensive shampoo.

They turned into the harbor, where seagulls flew in V-shaped configurations and boats with Dorito-shaped sails drifted along the emerald-green water. Where kids licked triple scoops of ice cream and kites danced through the sky. And where no one wanted to think about the biology of basic cells, ever. Ruthie included. But if Owen failed his test, she would be fired. And if she was fired, she'd never have enough money for a phone. Ruthie would remain socially obsolete and technologically challenged for the rest of her days. Like the old *Pilgrim* ship, she'd keel over in the middle of the night, never to be seen again.

"This looks like a good study spot," she said as they cruised past a park. If they sat at one of the picnic tables, Owen's spine would be straight, and his feet could be flat. It was an ideal posture for focus.

"The park?" Owen scoffed. "How are we going to kayak on the grass?"

"Kayak?"

Minutes later, Ruthie stepped into a wobbly kayak that was then shoved out to sea by the foot of a Harbor Water Rentals employee. It didn't matter how many times she told Owen their flash cards would get wet or that paddling would be too much of a distraction. He insisted. And as long as the customer was paying, he was always right.

"Just sit back and enjoy the ride, m'lady," Owen said in a cringy British accent. "I tend to get a little seasick, so it's best if I handle the oars."

Seated in the front with her fingers trailing in the cool water, Ruthie was instantly mesmerized by the sway of the boat, the slosh of Owen's paddle, and the diamonds of light that winked along the ocean's surface. Enjoying the ride was easy. That was what made this so hard!

"Most cells are made from a type of protoplasm," Ruthie shouted into the breeze. "What's it called?"

"Cookie?"

Cookie? Did Owen seriously think Swiss embryologist Rudolf Albert von Kölliker would name a type of protoplasm *cookie*? Did they even have cookies in 1863?

"Owen, we went over this on Friday. Is that really your best guess?" Ruthie turned around to find a Tupperware dish on the seat between them. It was filled with cookies that had been frosted with pink icing to read *Lana's First Love*.

"It's the name of the novel my mom's reading for her book club," Owen explained. "The woman's an obsessive monogrammer. She had tons of them made, so I swiped a few. Don't judge me."

Ruthie giggled and took one. The sugar went straight to her cells and made them hum. "Yum. What type?"

"Cytoplasm," Owen said.

Ruthie turned around again. "They're made with cytoplasm?" It was an alarming concept, but not one she would put past a mom who writes *Lana's First Love* on cookies.

"No, the type of protoplasm is called cytoplasm," Owen said. "I was answering your question."

"You *knew* that?" Ruthie asked, wishing she hadn't sounded so shocked.

"Yeah. We went over it on Friday. Remember?"

"Uh, yeah." Ruthie rolled her eyes at the ocean. Of course *she* remembered. "Okay, so what's the center of a cell called?"

"A nucleus."

"Yes!" Ruthie slapped the side of the kayak. "You're going to ace this! You might not even need my help in bio anymore."

"You think? I don't know. Ask me another one."

"The nucleus is the control center that directs all the cell's activities. It is surrounded by—"

"Hair."

"Hair? No. The answer is a nuclear membrane." Ruthie reached for a second cookie. Whatever Owen was paying her, it wasn't enough. "That's okay, you'll get this one. Inside the nucleus, there's a type of protoplasm called . . ."

"Sea lion!" he shouted. "Oh, no, wait, I think it's a trash bag. My old nanny looked like a sea lion." He stopped paddling. "Ugh, what was her name again?"

"Owen, what's the protoplasm called?"

"Rachel! That was her name. She looked like a sea lion. Or maybe it was a seal. I forget the difference."

"Sea lions are brown and have visible ear flaps.

Seals have small flippers and lack visible ear flaps," Ruthie managed.

"Oh, then it was definitely a sea lion. Rachel had sizable ears."

"Owen, I think we should return the kayak and study on land. It will be easier for you to focus and—"

A motorboat's engine buzzed. Ruthie paused to let it pass. When it did, a corduroy pattern of waves rolled toward the kayak, lifted it up, and smashed it back down. The impact was minimal and not at all scary. The splash, however, was enough to soak Ruthie's overalls and drench Owen's stiff side part.

Laughing, Owen shook it off like a wet dog. When he was done, vines of dark hair clung to his jaw and hung over his eyes. With the paddle across his lap and the sun warming his skin, he no longer resembled a pudgy Lego figurine. More like a rugged man of the land. Only on the water. And with a Tupperware full of *Lana's First Love* cookies instead of a slaughtered buffalo or a speared fish. Still, his hair was on point.

"What?" he asked as he ran a hand through his tousled vines. "Why are you staring at me like that?"

"Your hair . . . it's . . ."

"I know." Owen began smoothing it back into captivity. "It's unruly."

"No, stop!" Ruthie insisted. "You should keep it like that."

"For real?" Owen lowered his hand. "You don't think it makes me look . . . slovenly?"

Ruthie beamed. Of all the adjectives he could have chosen to describe his disheveled appearance, he picked that one. Her second-favorite word, after *oodles*. "I think it makes you look puissant."

Owen smiled like someone who knew the definition of *puissant*. "Why, thank you, m'lady." He plunged his paddle in the water and began turning the kayak.

"What are you doing?"

"You wanted to go back to shore."

"I have a better idea." Ruthie handed him the flash cards. "You study, and I'll paddle. It's a perfect day. Why rush?"

chapter sixteen.

"HAPPY MONDAY, POPLAR Middle," Principal Bell said over the loudspeaker. "As many of you know, there were several mishaps and misunderstandings with the seventh-grade field trip petitions last week . . ."

Fonda and Drew exchanged a giddy glance as they settled into their first-period seats. Henry's petition had been lost at sea, and if Sage's photobomb plan worked, the Avas, who probably spent the weekend overwhelmed by fake makeover requests, had forfeited. But not Fonda. She slapped her two-page petition on the school administrator's desk the moment the doors opened, and now Principal Bell was probably going to name her the victor.

". . . to ensure that every voice is represented, we

are going to hold a traditional election today during lunch . . ."

"NO!" Fonda shouted at the intercom. Then she turned a red-hot shade of mortified when everyone in language arts swiveled and glared.

". . . If you are in seventh grade, plan on eating in the gym. Each candidate will have two minutes to state their position, and then the ballots will be cast. The results will be announced at the end of the day. Go, democracy, and may the best idea win."

Hands shaking and breakfast churning, Fonda bolted to the bathroom for a self-pity cry. Her team worked hard for their signatures. Why was she being punished for her competitors' inability to cross the finish line? How was that even fair?

Fonda slammed the stall door, locked it, and held a wad of toilet paper to her face. Tears were about to fall and they, like her, deserved to be caught.

Just as the deluge began, the bathroom door kicked open and a familiar voice shouted, "No crying!"

"Sage?" Didn't TAG students have their own bathrooms? "What are you doing here?"

"As your campaign manager, it's important that I know where you are at all times."

"But how—"

"I put a tracking app on your phone. When that announcement ended, I was notified that you were en route to the bathroom. I knew you didn't have to pee. You went right before class."

Fonda unlocked the stall door, her insides heavy with unreleased tears. "What do we do now? I'll never win a vote against those two. Quitting is the only option."

Sage gathered her pink hair and twisted it into an efficient topknot. "How about you work on your attitude, and I'll work on your speech. Remember: when the going gets tough . . ."

Fonda rolled her eyes and mumbled, "The tough get going."

"No! The dumb-dumbs lose. Now get back to class and manifest confidence. I'll have something for you within the hour."

Voices were echoing off the gym walls, and sandwich smells thickened the air. A dense fog of panic was closing in on Fonda. At least the Avas were a no-show. It didn't *fully* alleviate Fonda's stress, but it helped.

"They must have dropped out," she told the girls as they escorted her to one of the three chairs behind the microphone.

"Super unfortunate, am I right?" Sage said.

Ruthie nodded. "Very right."

"Why is that unfortunate?" Drew asked.

Sage shrugged. "It would have been fun to beat them."

Laughing, everyone exchanged a high five except Fonda. She was too shaky to raise a hand, let alone aim it. Yes, Fonda had memorized Sage's speech, but could she deliver it? What if she froze midsentence? No one would ever want to join her friend group. And her sisters, who risked their reputations by endorsing Fonda on Instagram (Thank you, Inga Thornbird!), would never take her seriously again.

"Students, please take your seats and settle down," Principal Bell said. But the chatter continued to build as the entire seventh grade waited for Ava H. to arrive and fill the empty chair between Fonda and Henry.

Sitting stiffly, Fonda tried to review her speech, but Henry was speed-bouncing his feet and singing "Rap God," making anything other than wanting to punch him impossible.

Eventually, Principal Bell decided that the show must go on without Ava H. and stepped up to the microphone. She said some things about democracy and explained the voting rules. Then she introduced Henry. He shuffled toward her, enthusiastic as a kid on his way to do yard work. Still, he was met with enough whistles, woots, and claps to make Fonda question her entire existence. It didn't matter that Sage and the nesties were thumbs-upping her from the bleachers. Or that the TAG'ers were holding signs about the Catalina sea monster that read GET PAID FOR PEARL PICS! Unlike Henry, Fonda couldn't act too-cool-to-care. She cared way too much and had the sweaty pits to prove it.

"All of you have a slip of paper to cast your vote," Henry began. "But it's more than a slip of paper. It's a ticket to the future. A future that will teach you what it's like to be in the army with your buddies, only super fun. If you like paintball and ropes courses and surfing at San Onofre, choose Camp Pendleton today and have an epic tomorrow. Thanks." Henry's friends jumped to their feet and cheered while Henry ran a hand through his hair and shy-smiled like the humble guy he wasn't.

Principal Bell returned to announce Fonda when the gym doors pumped open.

"We're here!" Ava H. announced, as if that needed clarifying. She was flanked by Ava G. and Ava R. as they jogged across the gym floor, fists pumping like Laker Girls at halftime.

"Sorry we're late," Ava H. said into the microphone as she nudged Principal Bell aside. After a slight nod, Ava G. and Ava R. began unfurling a scroll that stretched from one end of the gym to the other. It contained all the awkward photos Sage had sent them—photos that were meant to overload their systems and cause their makeover idea to crash. Instead, they'd turned them into props.

Once the scroll and the girls were in position, Ava H. smoothed her brown lob and lowered her glossy lips to the microphone. "I have two words for you . . ."

She paused and leaned closer. *"Makeover."* Then she dropped the mic and sauntered off the stage while Ava G. and Ava R. ran around the gym, waving the photo scroll like a victory flag.

The applause was so explosive—and so un-deserved—it flipped a switch inside Fonda. What had once been dark was suddenly lit. If she was going to lose and be forgotten, why not be remembered for it?

Amid the applause, Fonda calmly picked the micro-phone off the floor and said, "Just so you know, Ava, *makeover* is one word, not two. If you want two words, try *Catalina Island*."

The nesties began jumping, Owen blew on his trumpet, and Fonda decided to abandon Sage's speech and wing it. These people didn't want brilliant rheto-ric and inspiring quotes about adventure. They didn't want fun facts about the buffalo that had inhabited the island since 1924. They wanted paintball, makeovers, and sea monster sightings. They wanted ice cream shops, spooky night hikes, zip lines, and surf spots. And Fonda promised it all.

When her two minutes were up, Fonda bowed to thundering applause. Even Sage, who had spent close to an hour perfecting a speech that was never used, seemed thrilled. Fonda's pitch appealed to all genders and all interests. She threw down like a hammer and nailed it.

✕

"THE FOLLOWING INFORMATION is for seventh-grade students only," Principal Bell announced at the end of last period—a period that seemed even more painful than the monthly kind Fonda's sisters often complained about. Granted, *this* period didn't have cramps or bloating, but it was full of heart-thumping anticipation and stressed-out nail-biting. It didn't matter how loudly the crowd had cheered for Fonda's speech; the ballots were cast anonymously. What happened behind those voting-booth curtains was anyone's guess. At least, it had been until now. Principal Bell finally had the results.

"After today's spirited lunchtime rally, it appears as though the new destination for the overnight is . . ." Principal Bell played a drumroll sound effect. Everyone found it charming except for Fonda's churning stomach and clammy palms. They desperately wanted her to get on with it. "Ferdink Farms! Just kidding, it's Catalina Island!" She went on about the importance of democracy, freedom of expression, and some other stuff that Fonda tuned out. Her ears only cared about the victorious squeals and high-five slaps that filled the classroom and spilled into the halls once they had been dismissed.

Hugs were exchanged, tears of joy were shed, and a victory party at Fresh & Fruity was scheduled for right after school. Were there a few minor details to sort out? Yes, but not today. Today was for celebrating. Surely, Fonda would figure out how to bring paintball, makeovers, and sea monsters to Catalina Island. They had two weeks! How hard could it be?

chapter seventeen.

DREW UNDERSTOOD FASHION well enough to know that beat-up skate helmets were not a thing. Still, she wore one as a personal reminder when they joined the line inside Fresh & Fruity. She was out of coupons and had dipped into her helmet savings fund twice in the past few weeks: once to buy that tragic green trucker hat and again to get Doug a costly slice of pizza he didn't want. Wearing the old helmet would remind her that she needed to save for a new one, and she'd say no-go to fro-yo. It was an odd but effective tactic. One that Fonda would never allow under normal circumstances. But there was nothing normal about that afternoon. A triumphant pack of seventh graders was at Fresh & Fruity to celebrate the nesties' win. It wouldn't have mattered if

Drew had been wearing a used diaper on her head; Fonda was too excited to care.

"Oh my frog!" Ruthie said as she took in the snaking line of bodies. "This place is a fire hazard!"

Owen blew his trumpet and bellowed, "The queen of Catalina has arrived!"

Leah Pellegrino began hyper-waving from the middle of the line. "Fonda, I made this for you!" She held up a purple-and-red pom-pom keychain. "Thank you for saving us!"

Everyone applauded. If the sudden attention made Fonda feel awkward or uncomfortable, she hid it like a pro. Golden-brown eyes glistening with gratitude, she glanced down at her leopard-print high-tops and said, "I couldn't have done it without your support."

"I still have my bling," Kat Evans called, proudly displaying her *I* ♥ *CAT* bracelet. "I never take it off. Not even for church."

Toni Sorkin added, "I'm still more of a dog person, but I'm super stoked for Cat Island! So are my traumatized nasal passages." Then she waved Fonda closer. "Come. Cut the line."

Fonda stepped forward.

Sage grabbed her by the arm and yanked her back. "Stay grounded."

"Huh?"

"You don't deserve special privileges just because you won. Doesn't *Qu'ils mangent de la brioche* mean *anything* to you?"

"Not really."

"'Let them eat cake,'" Ruthie explained. "Marie Antoinette said it in 1789 when she learned the peasants were starving and didn't have bread."

"What's so bad about cake?" Drew asked, tempted by the sugar smells wafting off the toppings bar. "It's better than bread."

"Hmmmm," Ruthie said. "Solid point."

Drew thought of Will. If only he had been there to hear her solid point. Maybe he would like her a little more—a little more than he liked Keelie. But why would Will be there? A bald man wouldn't go to a hairbrush party. It would only remind him of what he lost.

A gust of cool air entered the shop. *Will?* Drew whip-turned to find the Avas—each with a Fjällräven Kånken backpack slung over their shoulders.

"Ugh," Sage groaned. "Steppy alert."

"What are they doing here?" Fonda asked, her tone a mix of hope and fear.

"Probably demanding a recount."

"Nothing of the sort, nerd herder," Ava G. said in that high-pitched voice of hers.

Drew leaned closer to Sage. "How did she know what you just said?"

Sage covered her mouth and muttered, "She watches TV on mute so she can learn to read lips. Who's the nerd herder now, am I right?"

"We're here on official business," Ava H. said as they approached.

"We are? I thought you wanted to see if Henry was here."

Ava G.'s cheeks reddened. "What? No! We came to deliver *this*, re-mem-ber?" She handed the scroll of pictures to Fonda.

"Why are you giving it to me?"

"The beauty-challenged population at our school is huge. Huge and desperate. We tried to help, but in the end, they chose you. Which I totally get, by the way."

Fonda crinkled her nose the way Drew did when crop-dusted by a Doug fart. "You do?"

"Of course. They're intimidated by us. You're more . . . relatable. They *see* themselves in you."

Sage twisted her pink hair into a topknot. "You did *not* just say that!"

"I totally did. We're stoked to see what the Catalina makeover team does with the scroll girls. I mean, who doesn't love a makeover story?"

"Yeah," Ava G. said. "We're glad you guys are taking over for us. Helping people can be so draining." Then to Drew's helmet, "I'm surprised we didn't see *you* on that scroll."

The dig was so unexpected, Drew was unable to respond. She thought of Will again. Only this time, she was glad he hadn't been there.

But he was.

"Here you go, D," Will said, walking toward her with a cup of chocolate cream pie fro-yo topped with caramelized yuzu balls.

The harp music behind Drew's belly button started to play. *Have you been here this whole time? How did you remember my order? Are you wearing colored contacts, or were your eyes always this blue?* She wanted to ask all these questions and dozens more. But her thoughts kept bumping into one another and couldn't seem to find their way out of her mouth.

"That's for *me*?"

"A bet is a bet." Will handed her the cup and smiled.

Drew could barely feel her hand when she reached for it. The moment was too dreamy. The fact that he remembered their bet was one thing. The fact that he remembered the caramelized yuzu balls was ten other things—all of them amazing.

"What was the bet?" Fonda asked.

"Drew said you were going to win, and I said Henry would win. She was right. Anyway, it's pretty rad that you're going to get paintball on Catalina. How are you going to do that?"

Drew cut a look to Fonda. How *was* she going to do that?

"I was wondering the same thing about the makeovers," Ruthie said.

"And the sea monster," Owen added. "Is that a real thing, because I googled it and—"

"Henry!" Fonda called, welcoming the distraction. He was walking toward them with two cups of fro-yo and a sheepish grin. "For me?"

Ava H. rolled her eyes.

"Uh, no. I got two because the line was so long, I didn't want to wait for seconds."

Will gave Henry a nudge. "But you can have one if you want," Henry said. "You know, because you're gonna do the whole paintball thing."

"Thanks," Fonda said, no longer caring about special privileges or Marie Antoinette. Attention was her cake, and she was going to gobble up every bit of it. "What about Ruthie?" she asked, indicating Henry's other cup.

Owen lifted his palm. "At ease. I'll get Ruthie's and Sage's. Go and sit, m'ladies. You saved us from the Slopover, and now I shall save you from this undignified line."

"Well, enjoy," Will said with a goodbye wave.

"You're not staying?"

"Can't. Kallax is waiting for me."

The harp music stopped. He called Keelie *Kallax*? It wasn't the cutest nickname, but it certainly beat *D*.

"Why doesn't she come here?" Drew smiled, hoping to mask her jealousy.

"Kallax is not a *she*. Actually, it could be. I don't know. Are desks male or female?"

"Desks?"

"Yeah, Kallax is the name of the desk my mom got from Ikea. She's giving me ten bucks to put it together."

The harp music resumed.

"Yeah, well, it's not polite to keep a desk waiting," Drew said, then cringed a little.

"K, *well*, congratulations and, you know, nice helmet." He smiled. "You're going to need it for paintball."

"No, you are!" Drew fired back, then cringed again. Because what did that even mean?

What did any of this mean? All Drew knew for sure was that Will cared enough to honor their bet and remember her order. And that was good enough for now.

chapter eighteen.

RUTHIE WAS SITTING at Owen's bedroom desk, watching him pace. "What is the literary term for exaggeration?" she asked, desperate for him to focus.

He paused in front of his wall-to-wall fish tank. "Bowling!"

"No. The answer is hyperbole." *We've been over it a zillion times,* Ruthie wanted to say, along with *Did you notice I just used hyperbole?* But Owen had been sensitive lately. He got a fifty-two on last week's biology quiz, fifty-eight in math, and fifty-nine in American history. The guy needed patience, not scolding. And as long as Owen put the *pay* in *patience,* Ruthie would stay the course. The fact that he'd stopped shellacking his hair into a side part made it even easier.

"What I meant was, let's go bowling. I feel like a trapped animal in here."

"Great example of irony," Ruthie said, indicating the exotic fish that were quite literally trapped inside his aquarium.

Owen looked at her sideways. "I don't get it." He grabbed his cardigan off the hood of his race-car bed and slung it over his shoulder. "Anyway, the bowling alley has free shoe rentals on Wednesdays. Not that money is an issue. I mean, I can afford the fee—"

"This isn't about shoe rental, Owen. It's about preparing for your language arts test." The conviction in Ruthie's voice was undeniable. Yes, she wanted him to experience the joy of learning. But there was more. If Owen continued to get straight D's, Mr. and Mrs. Lowell-Kline would not only give her a terrible reference, they'd fire her.

"I have an idea," she tried. "Why don't we bowl *after* your test?"

"Borrrr-ing!" he said, as "Für Elise" began playing throughout the house.

"I think someone's at the door," Ruthie said, irritated by another distraction. She checked her pink cupcake watch. Her grumbling stomach had been right; it was almost dinnertime.

"Franklin and Eleanor are back from the dog spa!" Owen said, taking off down the hallway. "I shall return, m'lady!"

Ruthie lowered her head onto Owen's desk and banged four times—once for every bad grade he'd received under her tutelage, and one extra for the F he was about to get tomorrow if he didn't focus. Which he wouldn't. So now what?

Ruthie's father always said, "By failing to prepare, you are preparing to fail." Meaning: Owen would eventually persuade Ruthie to leave the house, and when he did, she'd have to be ready; quizzing him on the go was the only hope.

Ruthie opened the desk drawer in search of index cards but stumbled on a stack of tests instead—tests that she had never seen because Owen claimed to have ripped them up; he was *that* upset. Only these tests were very much intact. They were also incapable of upsetting Owen unless Owen had a problem with scoring 100 percent on ABSOLUTELY EVERYTHING!

"Oh. My. Cod!" Ruthie said. There had to be some

explanation. Some logical reason why she was tutoring Owen when he clearly did not need her help. What if the iridescent sea creatures in his aquarium had once been tutors, lured by the promise of money, then zapped by a laser and transformed into objets d'art? Why else would he be paying for a service he didn't need? Rich people loved collecting rare things, and what was rarer than a talented and gifted fish?

Ruthie shut the desk drawer and zipped up her backpack. A phone containing the numbers 9-1-1 would have been helpful. But, no. Her parents thought earning it was nobler. Well, how noble would it feel when they found her gills-up in a tutor tank?

Terrified, Ruthie hurried for the door and slammed straight into Owen.

"Where do you think you're going?" he asked, clutching a miniature rust-colored poodle under each of his arms. "Wait . . . why do you have your backpack?"

"Uh, my mom called," Ruthie blurted. "My uncle, the professional wrestler, stopped by with like five of his wrestler friends, and you know what they say about wrestlers . . . They always come looking for you if you're late for dinner."

"Seriously?" Owen asked.

"Yeah. They get super hungry."

"No," Owen said, frustrated. "Did your mom really call?" He set the dogs down on his bed. "When did you get a phone?"

"Uh, this morning."

"Why didn't you tell me?"

Ruthie swatted her hand like it was no big thing. "It's used. And broken. And it only accepts calls from my mother. I'm getting it fixed tomorrow. Nothing to brag about, trust me."

Owen held out his palm. "I'm good at fixing things."

"Yeah," Ruthie scoffed. "I bet you are."

"Thanks."

"I bet you're good at a lot of things."

"Thanks."

"Yeah. I bet."

Owen withdrew his hand. "Sorry, what's happening right now?"

"You're good at a lot of things. That's what's happening right now."

His cheeks reddened as he glimpsed the gold cup on his shelf. "You eye-spied my bowling trophy, didn't you?"

"No, Owen, I eye-spied the tests in your desk drawer!"

"Uh . . ." His red cheeks paled. "Yeah, about those . . ." He lowered onto the fender of his race-car bed and hung his head.

"Yeah, about those," Ruthie mimicked. "Are you trying to laser me into a fish?"

He lifted his face and laughed. Not a villain laugh, mind you, a friend laugh. As if her accusation was genuinely funny. Which, fine, it was.

"Why would I want to laser you?"

"I don't know! Why would you lie about getting straight A's?"

Owen stood; his smile waned. "You needed money."

"For a *phone*, Owen, not food."

He shrugged. "I wanted to help you."

"Help *me*? I was supposed to be helping *you*."

"You *did* help me."

"Wait." A new kind of sweat prickled the surface of Ruthie's skin. It was free of fear and full of pride. "You got those A's because of me?"

"No. I got those A's because I am the *gent* in *intelligent*." Owen slumped back down on the bed. "My IQ is 151."

"I don't get it," Ruthie said, which wasn't easy to admit. She reveled in her ability to get *it* and loathed when she didn't. "Why aren't you in TAG?"

"I have my reasons."

"Well, why do you need my help?"

"I don't. I just thought it would be fun to hang out."

Ruthie took a step back, feeling more suspicious than ever. "Why?"

"You know, you're cool, and—"

"Hold up!" Ruthie released her backpack to the floor. "You think I'm cool?"

Owen nodded. "The coolest."

This time it was Ruthie who blushed. That was the nicest thing a boy who wasn't her dad had ever said to her. "Owen, you don't have to pay to hang out with me."

"I don't?"

"No!"

"Really?"

"Is forty the only number spelled in alphabetical order?"

"It is indeed." He beamed.

"Then, yes, I want to be friends for free. Do you?"

"Is one the only number spelled in descending alphabetical order?"

"Indeed, it is." Ruthie beamed back.

"Then free friends we shall be."

An instant later, the realization of what had just happened settled in, and Ruthie's spirit began to deflate.

Owen placed a warm hand on her shoulder. "What's wrong? You look sad."

"Not sad," she sighed. "Unemployed. I don't have a used broken phone. I don't have any phone. And now I'll never—" Ruthie stopped herself. She didn't want to dump old problems on her new friend. She'd find another job somehow, someday. Right?

"I think I can help." Owen waved Ruthie over to his closet and opened its double doors with a magician's flourish. "Ta-da!"

Ruthie's jaw hung slack. This "closet" was the size of her bedroom. Only its shelves weren't bloated with time-worn puzzle boxes, books, and trophies. Instead, they displayed color-coordinated clothes that must have been folded by someone from the Gap. The creases were that precise. However, the real shelf de résistance was to the right and contained an Apple Store amount of phones, laptops, monitors, and headphones. "Where did you get all of this?"

"My parents. They feel guilty about working all the time, so they buy me stuff. And you want to know the weird part?"

"That's not the weird part?"

"No, the weird part is I don't use any of it. I'd rather read."

"How is that weird? I'd always much rather read."

Owen grinned. "I knew I liked you. As a friend, I mean."

"Obviously. And same," Ruthie said, even though his floppy hair and spectacular brain could make her susceptible to the crush virus . . . you know, someday, way, way down the road.

"Go for it," Owen said, indicating the shelf de résistance.

"Go for what?"

"Take whatever you want. The yellow one is the newest model. They weren't sure if I'd want that one or the red, so they bought both."

Ruthie extended her hand, then pulled it back.

"I can't. I have to earn it myself."

"Consider this logic," Owen said. "It's just going to sit there—waiting to be turned into landfill. Doesn't *Reduce, reuse, recycle* mean anything to you?"

Ruthie took a deep breath and considered this. It did seem wasteful to buy a new phone when a perfectly good one was sitting right there in front of her. "At least let me buy it from you."

"Why? It's not like I paid for it." He reached for his red phone, tapped the screen for a few minutes, asked her for the serial number of the yellow one, then, "Congratulations, friend. Your phone has been activated and all service fees have been added to my Friends and Family plan."

Ruthie expressed her appreciation so many times the words *thank you* started to sound like *thin-q*, which they agreed was a good name for a weight-loss app. They also agreed to keep their tutoring schedule so Ruthie's parents would think she was still working for her phone. It was dishonest, and she did feel bad about lying, but not as bad as she would have felt if she had to look for someone else to tutor, someone who wasn't her new friend Owen.

chapter nineteen.

VAN'S PIZZA PARLOR was surprisingly crowded for a sunny Sunday afternoon, the reggae music annoyingly upbeat. Bursts of laughter swelled and popped, then fizzled like fireworks. Dishes clattered, voices carried, and that peppy little bell over the front door cling-clanged incessantly. Fonda searched for the nearest exit. If she got up from the table and ran, she could be back in her room in twenty minutes. She could stress in peace.

This outing was all Drew and Ruthie's fault. They stopped by Fonda's house at twelve thirty and insisted she open the blinds, turn on some lights, get out from under her covers.

"Lunch at Van's?" Ruthie had suggested. "My treat!"

She flashed her new phone, reminding them that she no longer needed to save her tutoring money and had cash to burn, thanks to Owen.

"Not hungry," Fonda groaned.

"A change of scene will help you think," Drew insisted.

And she was right. A change of scene did help her think. She was thinking she should have stayed in bed.

"Pepper flakes?" the waiter asked as he placed three personal pizzas on their table.

"No, thank you," Ruthie told him.

"Ranch?" he asked. "It's not just for salad anymore. It's also a wonderful dip."

"No, thanks," Drew said.

"How's about some Parmesan? We have shredded, grated, and chunks."

Fonda's stomach roiled. On a good day, she thought Parmesan smelled like barf, and this was not a good day. Everything that could go wrong had gone wrong, and everything that could go right was also going wrong—including her pizza. "Um, excuse me? What are those green things?"

"Jalapeño peppers," the waiter said proudly. "And yes, they're organic. Every ingredient on the Spicy Vegan is sourced from local farmers markets."

"But I didn't order the Spicy Vegan. I ordered the Royal Hawaiian."

He began flipping through his notepad. "Says right here, two Sunday Funday thin-crust specials and one Spicy Vegan." He flashed a fake pity pout. It was infuriating.

"Well, *here* is not correct," Fonda snapped. She wasn't trying to be rude, but come on! She'd never even heard of the Spicy Vegan. She would have assumed it was an itchy skin condition, not a lunch option if she had.

The waiter adjusted his man bun. "I'll get that Royal Hawaiian out as quickly as possible," he told Fonda. Then to the others, "Bon appétit, now you may eat. Except you. You'll have to wait."

"It's okay. You can cancel it. I'm not that hungry."

"Don't cancel. She'll take it!" Ruthie told the waiter as he was leaving.

"If you don't eat it, I will," Drew said with a giggle. "Ha! I said *will*."

She was giddy and clearly very hungry from her

morning at the skate park, where she "coincidentally ran into Will" and "ended up riding next to him" for almost an hour. It was obvious that she wanted to analyze their "chance" encounter, break it down moment by moment, and really dissect it. But Fonda didn't have the patience for a crush convo. The Catalina Island trip was only eight sleeps away—and she couldn't deliver on any of her big promises. "Even if Sage *does* figure out how to make a sea monster hologram, we won't be able to see it in the daylight. It will be too bright."

"What if . . ." Drew slapped two slices of pizza together and took a giant bite. "We wait until dark."

"We won't be at sea in the dark. We'll be in our cabins."

"Then project the hologram by the cabins."

"A sea monster on land?" Fonda lowered her head onto the table. "I give up."

"Solid point," Drew said. "Hey, Ruthie, is it possible to see holograms in the daylight?"

No answer.

"Ruthie," Drew said again. "Ru-thie!"

Fonda lifted her head to find Ruthie staring at her phone, the corners of her mouth lifting into a smile.

"Dude!" Drew said with a flick to Ruthie's forehead. "Hello?"

"Owie! What did you do that for?"

"I was asking you a question."

"Sorry." Ruthie smiled, her eyes still fixed on her phone. "A cat is spinning around on a record player. It's hilarious!"

"I know, but Fonda needs our help. We have to focus."

The waiter appeared and placed a meat-covered pizza in the center of the table. "Sorry for the wait," he said. "The kitchen is really backed up today."

"What's this?"

"The Three Little Pigs," he said. "Pepper flakes?"

Fonda lowered her head again. "That's not what I ordered."

"Oops, my bad. This is for table nine. What did you want again?"

What do *I want?* Fonda thought. *I want Nanci from Catalina Island to tell me that she checked with her boss, and he said paintball is legal on the island. I want Sage to figure out how we will see a hologram in the daylight. And I want*

Lulu's makeup magicians to not charge me fifteen hundred
dollars per makeover because fifteen hundred times sixty is
impossible to calculate, let alone pay.

"She wants the Royal Hawaiian," Drew said. Then
to the girls, "Do you think Will thinks I was stalking
him? Because I wasn't. I was there with Doug."

"Why aren't you talking to him?" Ruthie asked. "He
bought you fro-yo. I thought you were all good."

"I said *stalking*, not talking. And we are good. I
think. I mean, we're not in a fight, but we're not really
friends either. We're somewhere between friends and
fight—we're *frights*."

"You have every reason to be afraid," Ruthie said.
"Stalkers are scary. Have you told your parents?"

Drew leaned across the table and yanked the phone
from Ruthie's clammy grip.

"What the heck?"

"You're not paying attention to, like, anything
we're saying."

"Give it back!"

"No!"

"Come on, Drew. Jerry's about to wakeboard!"

"So?"

"*So?* Jerry's a squirrel!"

"Well, we're your best friends, and we need you to focus—"

Fonda's phone started to ring. "Shhhh," she hissed. "It's Nanci!" She plugged one ear to block out the music and answered with a chipper "Hello?"

"Hello, this is Nanci with an *i* from the Catalina Island Tourism Board. May I please speak to Rhonda?"

"It's Fonda, actually."

"Oh, hello, Fonda. It's Nanci from the Catalina Island Tourism Board. I'm calling about your paintball inquiry. I'm sorry it's taken so long to get back to you. My boss had oral surgery on Thursday and wasn't picking up his messages . . ."

Fonda rolled her wrist, silently begging the woman to get on with it.

"What's she saying?" Drew whispered. "Can we do it?"

Fonda lifted a finger to her lips. *Shhhh.*

". . . I understand your seventh-grade class will be joining us for two nights," Nanci continued.

"Yes, and—"

Nanci exhaled. "Gosh, I just adore school groups. You know, my first visit to the island was on my seventh-grade field trip. Of course, that was a million years ago. But not much has changed. As you can imagine, I just fell in love with the place. So much so, that, well, here I am."

"Wow. That's so cool," Fonda said in that saccharine tone she saved for lonely grown-ups. "So, anyway, I was wondering if—"

"Becca, my eldest daughter, got married here last month. September is such a beautiful time of year. The tourists are gone, the weather is spectacular, and those monarch butterflies! Such miraculous creatures, aren't they? The way they transform themselves—"

"I know, right?" Fonda managed. "You know what else is transforming? Paintball. One minute your clothes are clean, and the next they're full of paint. It's so much fun."

Nanci snickered. "I feel sorry for whoever's doing the laundry when that's over."

Hope swelled inside of Fonda. "Does that mean we can do it?"

"Oh, no, dear. Absolutely not. Those pellets are a

real threat to our wildlife. But if it's adventure you're looking for, I'm happy to make some recommendations. For example, capture the flag—"

"Is there any way you can make an exception?"

"Hmmmm. I suppose if you lose the guns and the paint pellets, we will reconsider. Otherwise, dear, my hands are tied."

When the call ended, Fonda hurried for that exit. She had to get out of there before her friends started asking the kinds of questions that would make her cry in public.

It was official: Fonda couldn't deliver anything she'd promised. The whole grade was going to turn on her. She and the nesties were going to be outcasts. Hashtags like #FakePromises and #IHateCat were going to haunt her for life. If Fonda had had any idea that winning the election would turn her into a bigger loser than she already was, she would have quit while she was behind. But all she could do now was get back into bed, pull the covers over her tear-soaked face, and pray that her mother would let her switch schools.

chapter twenty.

THE EARLY MORNING sky was a lazy shade of blue. Much like the seventh-grade students waiting to board the Catalina Island ferry, it was half-asleep and trying to wake up. Still, the briny salt air crackled with excitement. For Drew it was more of a stomach-churning, anxious kind of excitement, because not only was this her first school sleepover, it was her first school sleepover with boys. And not just regular boys—*Will!*

It had been two weeks since he bought Drew a fro-yo, eight days since they ran into each other at Green Gates, and then seven days of meh. A passing wave here, a polite smile there; nothing more, nothing less. Their relationship status remained in the *fright zone*. And Drew hoped this trip would pull them out.

She glanced over her shoulder to evaluate Will's location. Approximately fifteen bodies stood between them. Sixteen, now that Sage had arrived with four hot chocolates and a pretty-please-with-whip-cream-on-top request to cut the line.

"What's with all the bags?" she asked. "Principal Bell said we could only bring one."

Fonda bit down on her thumbnail. "Yeah, well, PrinciBell doesn't understand the struggle."

Drew shot Sage a wide-eyed warning. *Don't say another word about Fonda's bags,* she silently urged. *Change the subject. Avoid confrontation. Let. It. Go.*

"Overpacking is a sign of insecurity," Sage stated. "And, Fonda, you have no reason to be insecure. Yes, you're a typical learner, but you're not a dumb-dumb." She took a sip of hot chocolate. "Clothes are easy to change, but few can change school policy the way you did. You are more than the sum of your outfits. Unlike *them.*" She hitched her thumb toward the parking lot, where the Avas were struggling to get their rolling suitcases to the dock. "Steppy and friends have been shopping for 'camping casuals' all week. Put that energy toward climate change or the fight against social injustice, not velour sweatpants and floral rompers, am I right?"

"No," Fonda said. "You're not right."

Ruthie finally looked up from her phone.

"Wait." Sage removed her glasses. "You think outfits are more important than human rights and the environment?"

Fonda rolled her tired eyes. "I meant, you're not right about my bags. They're not full of clothes."

"What, then?"

Deciding the conversation was over, Fonda scooped up her bags and dragged them forward as the line began to move. "You'll see."

"Water guns and makeup samples," Ruthie mumbled, mostly to her phone. "Because we can't do paintball or makeovers."

Sage slowly shook her head. "Tragic."

It was unclear whether she was referring to Fonda's failed promises or her so-so solutions. Not that it mattered. Drew had her own problems—Keelie and her SKATE HAIR, DON'T CARE hat were joining Will in line. What was Drew supposed to do now? Fake a butt dial so she had an excuse to talk to him? Beg Doug to drive back with *her* trucker hat? Spill hot chocolate on Will, then drag him away to clean him up?

"The good news is," Sage continued, "I solved the Pearl problem."

Fonda's expression brightened. "A daytime hologram!"

"No," Sage scoffed. "That's not a thing. I'm going to photoshop a picture of a sea monster into my ferry selfies, then post it."

"That's lying," Fonda said.

"Technically, so are holograms," Sage fired back. "And you were fine with those."

"Because we can see them. Photoshopping is straight-up fraud."

"This is politics, Fonda. Not polite-tics."

Fonda began nibbling her lip. The idea wasn't sitting well with her, and Drew understood why. Yes, Fonda wanted a high approval rating, but she didn't want to lie for it. And that was what Sage was asking her to do. It was also what Drew would be doing if she faked a butt dial, wore a copycat hat, or spilled hot chocolate on Will to pull him away. She wanted to earn Will's approval, not steal it.

"I don't know . . ." Fonda told Sage.

Drew, however, did know. She would put pride on the line and ask Will if he wanted to sit together on the ferry. No games. No politics. No polite-tics. Just straight-up honesty. No matter how he answered, Drew would be out of the fright zone, and her bravery would inspire Fonda. So much so, that paintball and makeovers and sea monsters wouldn't matter anymore. Courage would be the new cause, and Drew, its brave leader.

"Check out this sepia filter," Ruthie said as she held the phone in front of Drew's face. "It makes selfies look super old-timey."

"Be right back," Drew said. On the count of three, she stepped out of line. She counted to three again and took a deep breath. Then she turned toward Will and—

Keelie's hands were on his shoulders. Their eye contact was extreme. Their close talking, intense.

Drew accidentally spilled hot chocolate all over her sweats, then stepped back into line.

Up until now, she had questioned whether Will and Keelie were just friends. But their body language left zero room for doubt. It was official. They were in like.

The line inched forward, and reality set in. Drew wasn't the brave leader of the integrity movement. She wasn't inspiring others to put pride on the line and speak their truth. She was boarding a ferry that would take her to an island for three days and two nights, where she would have front-row seats to the *Will and Keelie Are in Like* show. After which she could binge-watch *Fonda Gets Taken Down by an Angry Mob of Seventh Graders*, and then maybe an hour or two of *Peeing in the Woods Was the Best Part of My Day*. Normally, Drew would have turned to Ruthie for support, but Ruthie was hunched over her phone, mesmerized by wacky animal videos and old-timey filters.

As they settled into their seats, Drew thought about faking sick and jumping ship, but the horn blew and the ferry's motor began to rev. There was no turning back now.

chapter twenty-one.

THE FERRY ROCKED and swayed. It tipped and tilted. Footsteps shuffled across the deck. Something was happening. Something exciting. Ruthie could feel a shift in energy; she could feel the salty breeze blow her hair. She wanted to look up. She needed to look up. She couldn't look up. She was playing Geometry Dash and had made it to Jumper—level seven, baby! Techno music was pumping. Her square was leaping. She was sticking every landing. Diving through every hoop. Avoiding every spike. Any and all distractions would have to wait. Level eight was right around the corner.

"What's happening?" she asked Fonda, eyes fixed on her phone.

Fonda didn't answer.

"Are we there?" Ruthie tried again.

Still no answer.

Ruthie sniff-sniffed, hoping for a whiff of Arm Candy—Fonda's vanilla-and-caramel-scented body oil. But the sniff did not have a whiff. *Where did she go?* "Drew? Are you here?" Ruthie paused for an answer that never came. "Sage . . . ? Owen . . . ?"

While her thumbs tapped wildly against the screen, Ruthie tried to recall the conversations she heard over the past twenty minutes. Had there been talk of switching seats? Did everyone disembark and leave her? What if Ruthie missed her stop and was heading back to Dana Point Harbor?

As far as she could remember, no one had said anything about leaving. She did, however, hear a boatload of angst.

"I swear if one more person asks me about Pearl, paintball, or makeovers, I'm going to walk the plank," Fonda had groaned. Then she added something about pretending to be asleep so no one would bother her. Ruthie hadn't heard her speak since.

At some point, Drew said, "I can't believe Will is sitting with Keelie."

And Sage responded, "Stop looking at them."

"I can't help it. Keelie keeps looking at *me*. I think she's checking to see if I'm jealous. It's so creepy."

"Said the creep who's checking to see if Keelie is checking. Come on, let's hit the snack bar. Oh, and start laughing when you stand up. Don't let her know you're jealous."

Then Owen appeared. "The snack bar's closed," he sighed. "Water's too choppy." He sat down beside Ruthie and peered over her shoulder. "Geometry Dash?"

"Yep. Almost done with level seven," she muttered. "Wanna watch me play?"

"Can't. I get super nauseous on boats. My mom gave me this acupressure bracelet. It's supposed to help with motion sickness—" The boat dipped suddenly. "Oh no . . ."

And that was the last she had heard from Owen. It was the last she had heard from any of them before the shift in energy. Something big was happening. But what?

Was Fonda walking the plank? Did Owen barf? Were Drew and Keelie fighting over Will? And if any of those things were happening to her friends, why was Ruthie just sitting there? Why wasn't she helping them? Why wasn't she taking pictures? Why wasn't she posting? #EverythingLooksBetterInSepia. #LifeAtSea #NestiesInLifeVesties . . .

Ruthie impaled her square on a spike and forfeited the game. The music stopped and her world went silent. Sunlight pinched the backs of her eyes. The sudden return to reality was shocking, disorienting.

Once her senses reacclimatized, she was overwhelmed by her surroundings—the glinting sea, the white seabirds, the magnificent arch of the island that was coming into view, and the vacant blue seats that had once been full. The boat dipped again. Everyone screamed.

Ruthie followed the terrified shrills to find the entire seventh-grade class moaning and clutching the railings. Those who weren't green were gray. Those who weren't hanging their heads over the water were writhing on the deck.

Owen simpered at the sight of Ruthie's ladybug socks. "Is that you, m'ladybug?" He was lying in fetal position, his skin the same color gray as his antinausea acupressure band. How ironic was that?

"Are you okay?" Ruthie asked.

"Seasick," Drew said on behalf of Owen. She was clutching her stomach.

"Sea monster?" Fonda called weakly. "Where?" Then she puked.

Ruthie, an expert on reading in the car during family road trips, was immune to the ferry's nauseating sway and decided to take a selfie. At least someone would have proof of their heroic crossing. You're welcome, yearbook committee.

While her classmates continued to moan and writhe, Ruthie positioned herself on the deck and framed her shot—island over her right shoulder, ocean over her left, and her smiling face in the middle. With an outstretched arm and an agile thumb, she switched the filter to sepia and—

A horn sounded. The boat lurched. Ruthie pitched forward. Her arm jerked backward. The phone slipped. And *SPLASH*...

"Nooooo!" she called as it vanished into the sapphire-blue water.

The engine cut, and the boat slowed to a stop.

"What's happening?" asked Ava G. as whitecaps slapped against the hull.

"I think we hit something," said Kat Evans, her enthusiastic ponytail bobbing with the boat.

"Look, everyone!" Fonda shouted, her voice no longer weak. With renewed energy, the entire seventh-grade class whipped out their phones just as a white-spotted gray beast, roughly the size of a school bus, glided by. "It's Pearl!"

"I call posting hashtag Pearl Harbor!" Keelie announced.

"We're not in the harbor anymore," Drew said. "This is the ocean."

Keelie rolled her eyes. "Looks like someone's jealous of my hashtags."

"Looks like someone *wants* me to be jealous of their hashtags," Drew fired back.

Normally, Ruthie would have high-fived Drew for defending herself. She would have applauded Fonda for spotting Pearl. And she would have asked to see everyone's pictures. But that was the old Ruthie—the light-hearted girl who celebrated her friends' victories. New Ruthie's spirits sank with her phone.

Now she was just a bitter, boat-hating, wave-loathing, ocean-despising, technology-free plebeian.

She couldn't even be bothered to marvel at Pearl, the sea monster. Because she knew it was a whale shark—a harmless, plankton-eating behemoth who probably took a wrong turn near Hawaii and ended up in Orange County by mistake. It didn't happen often, but it *did* happen. And the timing couldn't have been better. Everyone believed it was Pearl, and Fonda was basking in the glory of having delivered on one of her promises.

At least someone was happy.

chapter twenty-two.

"WELCOME TO CATALINA Island. My name is Nanci, with an *i*, and I'm here to make the next two days the best two days you've ever had! Woo-hooo!" She shot her fist toward the sunny sky, then straightened her straw hat.

The seventh graders cheered with delight. They were gathered on the dock, grateful to be back on land, and thrilled to have digital proof of the elusive sea monster. But Nanci wasn't fooling Fonda with her fun-loving welcome speech and safari-beige romper. Anyone who thought capture the flag was a reasonable substitution for paintball was fun-*hating*. So what if she had pink zinc on her nose? And double so what if she wore her hair in youthful side braids? Nanci was a Karen.

While she droned on about the island's delicate

ecosystem, the students secretly shared Pearl photos and flashed triumphant smiles at Fonda, smiles that seemed to say, *You made this happen! You're a miracle worker! Everything sucks!*

The everything-sucks smile was from Ruthie, and it looked more like gas pain. She was upset about losing her phone and probably felt left out. But, still. Pre-phone Ruthie would have been stoked to see Pearl pics, whereas post-phone Ruthie was standing there, arms folded, gaze down, as if ladybug socks were more impressive than water beasts.

"I can't believe we pulled this off!" Fonda whispered to Drew. Yes, she felt for Ruthie. But this was a moment for celebrating, not commiserating. She'd made good on one of her promises—the most unlikely one, at that! How could she not gloat? "I love that we didn't have to lie about Pearl," she said to Sage, rubbing it in a teeny bit.

Sage, not one for being wrong, held a finger to her lips. "Shhh. Nanci's talking."

Fonda rolled her eyes, then turned her attention back to Nanci, who was passing out itineraries. "As you're about to see, we have some super-duper activities planned, or at least I thought we did until Captain Briggs told me you saw a whale shark on the way over here." She knocked herself on the head with her papers and giggled. "I mean, who can compete with that?"

Fonda gasped; the sharp blast of air hit her lungs like a hatchet. *Whale shark? Was that even a thing?*

"Knew it," Ruthie muttered under her breath.

"You did?" Drew asked.

"Same," Sage interrupted. "The *Rhincodon typus* is my jam."

Ruthie high-fived her friend. "I had a feeling you figured it out."

"I had a feeling you had a feeling." Sage beamed. "What gave it away?"

"Who cares!" Fonda hissed, her entire social life flashing before her eyes. "Why didn't you tell me?"

"Why disappoint the dumb-dumbs?" Sage flicked her wrist. "Let them cling to innocence for as long as possible, am I right?"

"No, you're not right—"

"That wasn't a whale shark!" Leah insisted. "It was a sea monster!"

"Yeah, sharks aren't that big," Dune Wolsey said.

"Actually, dear, the average size of a whale shark is between eighteen and thirty-two feet. They typically live in tropical water, but now and then, one makes an appearance and—"

"You're saying that so you don't have to pay us!" shouted Kat Evans.

"Pay you?" Nanci snorted. "Why would I pay you?"

"For Pearl pics! It's your policy."

Nanci threw up her arms. "Who's Pearl?"

"The sea monster!" several students cried.

Toni Sorkin stepped forward. "I'm vice president of the student council, and I demand transparency."

"Kids," Nanci huffed, "I assure you, these waters are sea monster free, and we do not offer a sea monster *fee*." The parent chaperones chuckled at her corny turn of phrase. "How did this rumor get started, anyway? Surely, not your teachers."

"Fake News Fonda!" Keelie shouted.

Fonda's skin prickled with heat as everyone in the seventh-grade class glared at her.

"*You?*" Nanci asked with a hand to her heart. "Why?"

Fonda's body began to shake, and her mind went

blank. She didn't have a good explanation, and even if she did, she'd never find words to articulate it. "Uh . . ."

"Is this because I denied your paintball request?" Nanci pressed.

"No paintball?" Henry yelled.

"Seriously?" Will called.

Ava H. scanned the itinerary. "Why doesn't it say anything about the makeovers?"

"Or surfing at Shark Harbor?" asked Dune.

"Policy forbids surfing on school trips, dear," Nanci said.

Everyone began shouting at once, and Fonda started to quake. If she hadn't barfed her breakfast on the boat, she would have lost it right there on the dock. Her failure was epic and public and proof she'd never be as cool as her sisters, no matter how hard she tried.

Two hands touched her gently on the back. It was Drew and Ruthie, letting her know they were there for her. The gesture meant everything, but it did nothing. It was over.

She was over.

"Tell them about the water guns," Drew urged.

"And the makeup samples," Ruthie added.

Fonda was about to say something depressing like *What's the point?* or *No one cares*, when a high-pitched *whiz* sound distracted them. Everyone looked up to find a boy zipping by in a harness. "Wooo-hoooo," he called, his dangling legs bicycling overhead.

"Whoa," Henry said. "What is that?"

"A zip line," Nanci said proudly. "It goes around the entire island. It's one of the many activities you can sign up for."

"Looks rad!"

"We also have giant inflatable trampolines and water slides in the bay."

"Yes!" said Ava R. "What else?"

"Cliff jumping, rock climbing, and jewelry making with shells."

Everyone began shouting again, only this time they were elated.

"I want to do them all!" Ava H. announced.

"Me too!"

"Same!"

Nanci put her hands on her hips like Wonder Woman. "That's what I'm here for. Sign up for as many as you want!"

"I thought we were going to learn things," Sage said.

"You are. We offer late-night breakout sessions while you sip hot chocolate and eat s'mores by the campfire."

Before long, the jeers turned to cheers morphed into a praisefest for Fonda, the nesties, and their awesome overnight. Right when Fonda thought it couldn't get any better, Nanci made an announcement.

"You have thirty minutes of free time before lunch," she said. "You can use it to explore the local boutiques, jump in the ocean, or check out the campsite. Just don't fill up on ice cream or candy at the Sweet Spot."

But of course, that's precisely what they did. And it was delicious.

chapter twenty-three.

DREW REACHED FOR a red grip, pulled herself up a little higher, then paused to admire the shell friendship bracelet she, Ruthie, and Fonda had made. *This one is special,* she thought as she Spider-Woman'ed her feet onto the pegs of the rock wall. It proved that when the nesties worked together, they could accomplish anything. Well, almost anything. Will was still ignoring her.

"Why did I agree to this?" Ruthie shouted over the pop music that was blasting in the boulder gym. She was only two feet off the mat, and her forehead was already glistening.

"It's good exercise," Drew called down to her.

"*This* is inhumane. My arms are literally shaking."

"At least you have arms," Sage whimpered. "My bones have liquefied. I'm all skin."

Fonda suddenly appeared beside Drew. "I totally know why you wanted to do this," she panted. "And for the record, I have mixed feelings about it."

"What do you mean?" Drew asked, trying to sound innocent.

Fonda flicked her chin toward the arching ceiling, and Will, who was only a few feet away from ringing the victory bell. "If you want to stalk, stalk. I just wish you didn't rope me into it. Actually, a rope would be good. If I fall—"

"If you fall, you'll land on the mat, and I'm not stalking," Drew insisted. "I boulder all the time at Battleflag. Ask Doug."

"If I don't die, then yeah, I'll ask Doug. And if I do die, it's because you're a stalker."

"Shhh," Drew hissed. "The walls have ears." And she didn't want them to hear she had dragged her friends to a boulder gym because Will was there. They would think Drew was holding on to some pathetic fantasy, one where Will saw how athletic she was and chose her over Keelie. And they would be right.

"At least you-know-who isn't here," Fonda whispered. She was referring to Keelie, and yeah, Drew was well aware of her absence. "You think they broke up?"

"Dunno." Drew placed her hand on a yellow peg and hoisted herself higher, like someone who didn't get a tingle at the thought of the *Will and Keelie Are in Like* show getting canceled.

"Is everyone having fun?" Fonda asked for what must have been the ten billionth time. Her hands were practically raw from all the high fives. And yet she still wanted reassurance. What was it about happiness that felt too good to be true?

"Everyone is having a blast," Drew told her again. "Even Ruthie."

"Yeah, she's only mentioned her phone six times since we got here."

Drew laughed. "I still think she's having fun."

"Help!" Sage called. "I get dizzy when I look down."

"Then don't look down!" yelled Owen.

"He's right," Ruthie said. "Keep looking up."

"How do you know that guy?" Sage asked.

"He's my friend." Ruthie giggled. "He goes to our school."

"Oh, I wondered why he was following us."

"I'm not following anyone," Owen said. "I'm leading. Try to keep up, will ya?"

Drew sighed. He said *Will*.

Then, a second later, Henry said *Will*. As in, "Will, get your butt out of my face!"

To which Will responded, "Dude, get your face out of my butt!"

Laughing, Henry began to lose his footing. "Uh-oh," he said, sliding. "I can't hold on!"

In a shocking act of heroism, Fonda reached for Henry's swinging leg and tried to place it on a grip. The sudden gesture threw him even more off balance, which threw Fonda off balance, and they both plummeted toward the mat.

Drew shut her eyes, bracing for the worst. As a wannabe nurse who devoted much of her summer to helping out in the camp's infirmary, Drew was skilled in the art of wound dressing and scrape cleaning—but broken bones and concussions? Not so much. Fortunately, the worst never came. Henry and Fonda landed in the center of the mat and started cracking up.

"Are they okay?" Sage called.

"Don't look down!" Owen warned.

"Oh no!" Sage moaned. "I'm going timber." She landed on the mat with a *thunk*.

"Right behind you!" Ruthie shouted.

Owen jumped. "I'll save you!"

Before long, all five of them were rolling on the mat, laughing themselves breathless. "This is way better than Pendleton!" Henry said.

Drew warmed at the sight of the different friend groups coming together and bonding. It was what Fonda had always wanted; it was what *she* had always wanted. Sort of. She and Will were still clinging to their grips, the only two not laughing.

"Henry was right, this is more fun than Camp Pendleton," Will said while making his way down the wall. He didn't bother marking his victory by ringing the bell, probably for the same reason Drew stopped climbing. The top no longer felt like the place to be. Together did.

"Have you done the zip line?"

"No," Drew said, hoping he couldn't hear her speeding heart. "You?"

"Not yet." Will shimmied down beside her. "Wanna try it with me?"

"Aren't you going with Keelie?"

Drew regretted the question the instant it shot from her mouth. Could she have sounded any more jealous?

"No, Keelie's afraid of heights . . ."

Panic prickled. Was she the backup?

"Which is fine," Will continued. "Because, no offense to Keelie, but I'd rather zip-line with you."

Drew's clammy hands became sweaty. "Huh?"

"I said—"

"I heard what you said; I just don't get it."

Will scoffed. "What don't you get?"

"Aren't you and Keelie a thing?" Drew asked, no longer caring if she sounded jealous. She *was* jealous. And the sooner she knew the truth about Will and Keelie, the faster she could jump down from the wall, run to the bathroom, cry to her friends, eat frozen yogurt, cry again, eat more yogurt, then start to heal.

"What kind of thing?" Will pressed.

Drew shrugged. "A thing-thing."

He smiled, amused. "No."

The flutter of harp music behind her belly button returned. "You don't like Keelie?"

"I do like her. But I don't like-like her."

"You don't?"

"No. I like-like someone else."

"Who?" Drew dared.

Will lowered down a little. "I'm not telling."

"Come on, give me a hint."

"Fine. Her name sort of rhymes with *flea*."

The harp music stopped. "It *is* Keelie."

"No it's not!"

"I saw you close-talking on the boat," Drew pressed.

"Yeah, well, what do you think we were talking about?"

Drew shrugged.

"I didn't know if Flea liked me or like-liked me, and Keelie told me to straight-up ask her."

"Well, did you? Who is it?"

"I told you, her name rhymes with *flea*."

More guessing games? Really? "Whatever, I give up."

Will lowered down a few pegs, then looked up at her with those denim-blue eyes and said, "Her name is D."

The harp music returned. Maybe that nickname wasn't so bad after all. "Wait. What?"

"*D* rhymes with *flea*," Will said.

"It's *me*?"

"Yeah, that rhymes too. But, yes. It's you."

"Oh." Drew turned away so he wouldn't see her blush. The sudden movement, combined with the sweat on her palms, made her lose her grip and smack down on the mat beside the others.

"Incoming!" Will called, and then he jumped down and landed beside Drew.

"Do you like-like anyone?" he whispered, probably so their friends, who were lying beside them, laughing, wouldn't hear.

How could you even ask me that? Isn't it obvious? Drew wanted to shout. But all she could do was pretend she didn't hear him. Responding in front of everyone would have been embarrassing. And falling off the wall because of her sweaty hands was embarrassing enough. Instead, Drew took pleasure in knowing that their crush conversation was far from over and gave in to the laughter.

✕

DURING DINNER, DREW told her friends all about the rock talk she had with Will. When she got to the part where he asked her how she felt, Fonda demanded change.

"Speak up and put an end to the oppression!" she insisted.

Drew smirked. "Oppression?"

Fonda bit into a French fry. "You have been kept down for too long. Make yourself heard!"

"This isn't a political rally. You know that, right?" Ruthie said. "Drew's talking about testing positive for the crush virus. And she would have made herself heard if she had some privacy. Right, D?"

"Exactly," Drew said, smiling at her new nickname.

"*Life* is a political rally," Fonda declared. She had gotten a taste for changing the system and obviously liked it. Her mother would be proud. "Now, rise up and fight!"

"What does that even mean?" Sage asked.

"It means she has to tell Will if she's one like or two." Owen placed a hand on Drew's shoulder and nodded. "No more shyness. Own your feelings. It's time."

After dinner, Drew spent her free period and five dollars of her helmet money on a cup of pecan praline fro-yo topped with peanut M&M's and almonds, then delivered it to Will as they settled around the campfire.

"For me?" he asked. The sun was setting behind him. As it slipped below the horizon, Drew thought of a coin dropping into a piggy bank. Everything in its orange-colored wake had one last chance to matter before the opportunity fell away.

"I was thinking about what you asked me at the boulder gym," Drew began. This was super awkward. The entire grade was nearby. She looked down at her UGG boots, her nervous wiggling toes. "And . . ."

"Yeah . . . ?" He wrapped both hands around the fro-yo cup and held it like a prayer.

"Here." Drew handed him a plastic spoon. "I hope you *like*-like it."

This time it was Will who looked down. "I do like-like it," he said. Then he lifted his gaze, found hers, and joked, "I'm nuts about it."

"Yeah." Drew giggled. "Me too."

chapter twenty-four.

ON PAPER, THE first day of the field trip had been perfection. Ruthie saw a whale shark, ate fro-yo before lunch, made a new friendship bracelet, bounced on water trampolines, almost climbed a boulder wall, learned about the constellations, and laughed her abs off. But this wasn't paper. It was real life. And in real life, one could have everything and still feel like something was missing. Especially when that something was resting at the bottom of the Pacific, along with Ruthie's only hope of becoming relevant in the twenty-first century.

On paper, day two was off to a great start. They had chocolate chip pancakes for breakfast and were now on the beach, suiting up for a midmorning snorkel. But as real life would have it, there was only one size-five flipper in the bin. Which was fine. Ruthie didn't want to snorkel anyway. Her heart was so heavy she'd probably sink. All she could do was gaze out at the horizon and sigh.

"What's wrong now?" Sage asked, her lips stretched wide from the mask.

"The ocean." Ruthie sighed again. It wasn't that she wanted to mope, it was that she didn't know how to stop. "It's triggering."

"I know you're bummed," Drew said as she wiggled her foot into a flipper. "But maybe losing that phone was a good thing. You were kind of addicted."

"Maybe."

Ruthie secretly disagreed, but she didn't see the point in arguing with a girl in like-like. Drew was glass-half-full about everything now that she and Will had tested mutually positive for the crush virus. And Ruthie's glass had been shattered.

"Drew's right." Fonda sprayed her legs with sunscreen. "You were a library book on that thing."

"A library book?"

"Yeah, checked out."

The girls' snorkels bounced as they nodded in agreement.

"Maybe," Ruthie said again. Though this time, they were right. She was checked out. The allure of a device that delivered world news and endless animal videos could not be denied. But that allure would have worn off eventually. She would have learned to control her usage. And if she didn't, weren't there apps for that? Not that it mattered. It wasn't like Ruthie was getting another phone. Ever. The only job she qualified for turned out to be fake.

"I'm just coming to terms with the fact that I'm going to be deviceless and disconnected for the rest of my life. Maybe even longer."

"Let's go in the water!" Drew enthused as she and the others began flipper-marching into the ocean. "It will take your mind off things."

"Okay, be right there," Ruthie said. She made a show of rummaging through the bin for another flipper, but really, she needed a minute alone.

If only she had Foxie, the stuffed fox she kept behind her bed. Foxie was her confidant, the one she talked through her secret uglies with, uglies so ugly she wouldn't even share them with the nesties. And right now, her debilitating self-pity felt ugly.

Once everyone was in the water, Ruthie sat against a rock and drew a picture of Foxie in the sand.

"I'm ashamed of how pouty I've been," she told the Foxie proxy. "But I can't stop feeling sad."

Are you sure this is about the phone and not something else? the Foxie proxy would have said if it talked.

Ruthie looked out at the ocean and the clusters of black tubes poking through the water. Her classmates were learning and exploring—two of her favorite things—and she was on the sidelines. Why?

She leaned her head against the rock, closed her eyes, and considered her answer. The sun felt comforting on her face—a warm reminder that some things would always be there.

"Maybe this isn't about the phone," she told the Foxie proxy.

Go on . . .

"Maybe it's about shame."

How so?

"I didn't earn the money to buy it, I couldn't keep

it safe, and I didn't tell my parents about it. The whole thing was an epic fail, and I'm not used to failing."

Failure is an integral part of being human. It's how we learn.

Ruthie smiled a little—a sand drawing of a fox talking about being human . . . Ironic, much?

"It's time!" Owen announced as he flipper-marched out of the ocean and hobbled toward her.

Ruthie quickly erased Foxie. "Time for what?"

Owen lifted the mask away from his face. There was a red ring around his eyes that might have looked dorky to some, but Ruthie found it endearing. "I've been charting the tides and observing the currents, and if the subwater sand patterns are saying what I think they're saying, your phone would have washed ashore this morning at roughly nine forty-seven a.m."

Ruthie stood. "That's impossible."

"Actually, it's quite probable." He squinted up at the sky and drew an imaginary line from the sun to the ocean, and from the ocean to the beach. "It's over there!"

Ruthie followed Owen to a fly-infested heap of seaweed, where he dropped to his knees and started digging. There was no way. But what if there was . . .

"Voilà!" he said, pulling a phone out of the oily green tangle.

"Oh my log!" The moment was too glorious to consider how a phone that weighed close to seven ounces could dislodge from the ocean floor and get swept so far, so fast. And even if it could, would it work? Whatever. Logic was for later. All Ruthie cared about now was getting that beautiful red rectangle back in her hands and—

"Wait." She paused. "That's not my phone."

"Of course it is."

"No, mine was yellow, and this one is . . ." Ruthie swatted a fly. "This one is yours!"

Owen lowered his head. "Guilty as charged."

Ruthie stomped back to her rock and sat. How dare Owen fill her with false hope and then deflate her? And double how dare he play her for a fool?! Did he really think she'd buy the physics of that ridiculous story?

As he flipper-marched toward her, head still low, Ruthie decided that forgiveness wasn't an option because she wasn't mad. She was grateful. Owen had concocted an elaborate, albeit ridiculous story for her. And that alone cheered her up.

"Take it," he said, offering his phone.

"I can't."

"You can. I have six more."

"No, I mean I can't because I don't want it. The smartphone was turning me into a dumb-dumb."

"Ironic, much?" he said.

"Ironic very much." Ruthie beamed. Finally, a friend who valued literal opposites as much as she did! "Can you please tell me why you never tested to be in TAG? You're kind of a genius."

Owen folded his hands across his cute pudgy belly. "Kind of?"

"Fine, you're a total genius. Why aren't you in the program?"

"It's a tight group, and I'm not a fit-in type of guy."

"That's the second-dumbest thing you've ever said. You have been fitting in ever since we got here. You're one of us now, whether you like it or not."

"When you say *us*, do you mean your nesties or your Taggers?"

"I mean my friends."

Owen's eyes got a little watery. He turned away

from the sun. "What's the first-dumbest thing I've ever said?"

"Subwater sand patterns," Ruthie teased. "Is that even a thing?"

"Of course it's a thing." He turned back toward her, offered his hand, and pulled her up to stand. "I'll show you."

And off they went.

chapter twenty-five.

THE PALM OF Fonda's right hand still stung from the countless high fives she received earlier on the ride back to Dana Point Harbor. Though painful, its sting was a glorious reminder that Catalina Island had been a huge success, Fonda was responsible for that success, and everyone knew it.

"Is that your mom's car?" Leah Pelligrino asked Fonda as they disembarked the ferry. They were dragging their bags, and themselves, to the parking lot—tired but triumphant after their action-packed adventure.

"Where?" Fonda quickly removed the yellow sunglasses she'd "borrowed" from Amelia on the off chance that Leah was right.

"There." Leah pointed at the red Prius. "I wonder if Amelia's using the triple-pom keychain I gave her."

Adrenaline zipped up Fonda's spine. Something must have happened to her mother. "And I wonder why they're here."

Without another word, Fonda hurried toward the Prius.

"What is it?" Fonda asked. "Did something happen to Mom?"

Barefoot, Winfrey got out of the car and popped the trunk, the coconut scent of her leave-in conditioner leading the way. "You mean Joan?"

Fonda nodded. How many mothers did they have?

"Joan's fine," Winfrey said. "A little preachy, but fine. Why?"

The passenger door opened, and Amelia emerged. "Hey, how was the trip? Need help with the bags?" Her mirrored sunglasses reflected Fonda's confusion. Why were they here? Why were they talking to her in public? Why were they being so . . . unmean?

Winfrey grabbed Fonda by the wrist. "Cool bracelet. Are those real shells?"

"Yeah, we found them on the beach."

Amelia twisted her wild auburn curls into a top-knot. "Did you snorkel?"

"Yeah."

"Zip-line?" Winfrey asked.

"Uh-huh," Fonda said, still suspicious.

"Jump on the water trampolines?"

"Twice."

"Climb the boulder wall?"

"Sort of." Fonda smiled at the memory of her friends lying in a heap on the mat, laughing.

"How about that epic candy shop?" Winfrey narrowed her cactus-green eyes. "What was the name of it . . . the Hot Spot?"

"The Soft Spot," Amelia tried.

"The Sweet Spot," Fonda said.

"Yes, that's it!"

Winfrey high-fived Fonda. The pain was searing. "What's with all the questions?" she asked, blowing on her palm. She wanted to revel in their sudden interest, roll around in it like a dog on a field of fresh-cut grass. But she resisted. It had to be a trap. "Why do you care so much?"

"Dunno," Winfrey said. "It's been quiet with you gone, I guess."

"And it's cool how you made the whole thing happen," Amelia said. "I wish someone had saved us from Ferdink Farms."

"Same," Winfrey said. "Hey, who wants to celebrate with a tower of Stack's pancakes?" She flashed her mother's debit card. "Joan's buying!"

Fonda glanced at the sky, tempted to thank whoever was responsible for her sisters' newfound respect. Instead, she stopped and thanked herself. She was the one who fought for change, then risked everything to get it. The credit belonged to her. Not some heavenly force or stroke of luck. So, yes, Fonda was going to celebrate, just not with them.

"Stack's sounds fun. Maybe some other time," she said in her kindest voice. "I'm celebrating with my friends."

"You mean Drew and Ruthie," Amelia snipped.

"Yes," Fonda said proudly. "And a few others. You can meet them if you want."

Before they could respond, the nesties, along with

Sage, Owen, Will, and Henry, appeared by Fonda's side.

"We're thinking of staying at the harbor," Henry said. "You in?"

"There's a sno-cone truck," Drew said.

"We can rent stand-up paddleboards," Ruthie said.

"And kayaks," Owen added.

"Rent?" Fonda glanced at the debit card in Winfrey's hand and widened her eyes.

After a sharp exhale, Winfrey gave her the card. "Fine."

Fonda wanted to hug her sister but didn't want to risk ruining the moment. Instead, she kept her cool and introduced her new friends. Then she braced herself, expecting Sage to fawn over their style and the boys to fall in love with them, forgetting Fonda ever existed.

"Hey." Sage waved.

"Sup?" Will mumbled.

"Pleasure," Owen said, though he didn't look overly pleased.

Henry didn't say anything. He simply lifted his palm, then turned back to Fonda. "Are you in?"

It was as if Winfrey and Amelia were just two regular people and Fonda was the only Miller that mattered. "Totally." She beamed. "Let's go."

Her days of being a tagalong were finally over. Fonda was a be-long now. The future was so hers.

acknowledgments.

If you're the type of person who reads the acknowledgments, you will notice that the following names are also at the end of *Girl Stuff*. That's because these people showed up again for me and, as always, brought their A game.

Thank you, Jennifer Klonsky, president and publisher at Putnam Young Readers, and Jen Loja, president of Penguin Young Readers. This book would be a very long blog post without you.

Thank you to my longtime collaborators at Alloy Entertainment: Josh Bank, Sara Shandler, and Lanie Davis. Ready for another one?

Thank you to the dealmakers: Richard Abate, my agent, who, after eighteen years, still manages to have better hair than I. Thank you, James Gregorio, my patient contract lawyer. Thank you, Romy Golan, for getting these books into foreign countries and keeping us all on schedule.

Thank you, Olivia Russo, Christina Colangelo, Kara Brammer, Carmela Iaria, and Alex Garber, for your PR and marketing genius.

Thank you, Jessica Jenkins and Judit Mallol, for this fabulous cover. Thank you, Suki Boynton, for making the inside look equally fabulous. And a massive thank-you to copyeditor Ana Deboo and proofreaders Jacqueline Hornberger, Ariela Rudy Zaltzman, and Cindy Howle for making you think I am an English-language savant. I am not. *They* are.

Thank you, Caitlin Tutterow, for making it all run so smoothly.

Thank you, Xbox, for keeping my wonderful sons, Luke and Jesse, busy so I can write. And a billion thank-yous to my parents, Shaila and Ken Gottlieb. Probably the only two people who have read this far. I take that back. No way my dad did. (Thanks, Mom.)

Off to write another . . .

Xoxo Lisi

THERE'S ALWAYS MORE GIRL STUFF!

Fonda, Drew, and Ruthie have been besties forever, but there's nothing like seventh grade to test the bonds of friendship. Can they survive the challenges of crushes and cliques?

girl stuff.

lisi harrison

#1 BESTSELLING AUTHOR OF THE CLIQUE SERIES

The besties want to have their first kisses
on the same night, but it turns out some
moments just can't be planned. Who knew
boy stuff could be this complicated?

awkward stuff.

a *girl stuff* novel

lisi harrison

#1 BESTSELLING AUTHOR OF **THE CLIQUE** SERIES